1395/10 46

P9-BTN-346

Dove Dream

Dove Dream

Hendle Rumbaut

Houghton Mifflin Company
Boston 1994

The legend of the moon maiden and the prairie flowers in Chapter 6, pp. 40–42, is adapted from "When the Stars Took Root" in *When the Storm God Rides: Tejas and Other Indian Legends,* retold by Florence Stratton. Scribner's, 1936.

Library of Congress Cataloging-in-Publication Data

Rumbaut, Hendle.
  Dove dream / Hendle Rumbaut.
      p.   cm.
  Summary: In 1963, having come to live with her young aunt in the Kansas countryside while her parents sort out their problems, a thirteen-year-old Chickasaw Indian girl nicknamed Dovey ponders her past and her future.
  ISBN 0-395-68393-9
  1. Chickasaw Indians — Juvenile fiction.   [1. Chickasaw Indians — Fiction. 2. Indians of North America — Kansas — Fiction. 3. Kansas — Fiction. 4. Aunts — Fiction.]   I. Title.
PZ7.R8876Do   1994   93 — 26538
[Fic] — dc20   CIP
                          AC

Printed in the United States of America

BP   10   9   8   7   6   5   4   3   2   1

To my Dad,
William Biklen Pendleton

Also, thanks to a great editor,
Margaret Raymo

Dove Dream

· 1 ·

Anna and I sped down the long country road, kicking up thick clouds of dust behind us. It was especially hot that summer in Kansas, and my parents were on the verge of another breakup. It was 1963, and I was thirteen. I had been told that I would be living with Anna until school started again.

Something by Bobby Vee was blasting from the radio, and Anna sang loud harmony in her chronically hoarse voice.

"But the ni–i–i–i–ght has a thousand eyes," she wailed, her vibrato heavy, *"and a thousand eyes can't help but see —"*

Her long red scarf blew straight back from her thick black hair, and, when I looked at the speedometer, I was thrilled to see we were going fifty. On this road it felt like eighty. My parents would have had a conniption.

Anna was vital, independent, courageous, her foot

always pumping the accelerator of life — the exact opposite of my weak, confused parents. Mama was usually sick; Daddy, when he was around, was brooding and out of work. I could tell that this summer was going to be an adventure.

"So, remember, when you tell those little white lies," she sang, looking over at me. *"That the night,"* we sang together, *"has a thousand eyes."*

The road, basically straight, suddenly made a veer that Anna wasn't ready for. I shifted sharply to the left and slammed into her side. This was before seatbelts or sensible speed limits. Her body was strong, yet soft. I wished I were younger, so I could cuddle up next to her. But Anna didn't seem especially the cuddly type; she was single, a fighter for causes, a righter of wrongs. She was also my only aunt.

"Ever notice," she said, turning down the volume only slightly, "how big the sky seems once you're out of town?"

"Mmmmm," I said, looking up at the vast blue sky filled with clusters of huge popcorn clouds.

Of course, my family seldom left Lawrence, so I hadn't had much experience in that department. My early natural gypsy urges had been quelled, since I had to live at home, and be my mother's caretaker.

Suddenly I realized we were past the usual stretch of Highway 59, and I didn't know where we were. A glorious chill enveloped me, as though we were going on a long trip, though it really wasn't that far away.

"Where are we going, Aunt Anna?"

She laughed and blew a wad of Juicy Fruit out of the window.

"Going?" she echoed. "Why, I don't know, dear. We're just driving and driving. Isn't it fun?"

"Yes, ma'am," I said earnestly. "It's the best fun I've had."

"Ma'am!" she wailed. "Just Anna will do nicely, my little dove." She always called me that, or Dovey. Never my given name, Eleanor Ruth. It was another reason for liking her; she knew I wasn't an Eleanor Ruth.

"Sorry," I said, giggling. "It's just that —" I looked down at my knobby knees. My stomach gurgled softly. Maybe from the hamburger I'd eaten before we left.

"Oh," she said, shaking her head, "it's not your fault. That's how you've been brought up. With all their 'sirs' and 'ma'ams.' But that makes life stiff, don't you think? Like a corset."

I nodded. My white friend Wendy's grandmother still wore one, though they were mostly out of fashion. Every morning Wendy had to help her lace up; they called it "roping the calf."

Anna laughed and threw back her head. The golden wheat fields waved back and forth in the wind, the highway cutting them down the middle like the parting of the Red Sea.

Here and there were little farms with white wooden houses, children in the yard, a tractor plowing up the field. A group of horses galloped near the fence on the right. My heart raced as it always did when I was around horses. I loved everything about them — their size, their warmth, the power I felt as I rode on their sensuous backs. But riding had become a forbidden pleasure since I'd fallen last year and broken my arm.

Anna came to a screeching halt and pulled off the road, her eyes lighting up. "There's Walter!" she shouted. She picked an apple from one of the three bags of groceries on the back seat and got out.

The horse was enormous. His sweaty back shimmered in the fading afternoon light and he went right up to Anna and ate from her hand. Then she let me give him bites from what was left. We just stood there staring silently for the longest time at his glorious face and friendly brown eyes, his long white teeth.

"Isn't he something?" asked Anna. "Such a magnificent creature. Oh, you must ride him this summer."

"I'd love to, Anna, but —"

A farmer in a pickup truck was slowing down and honking at us. He leaned out the window and smiled. "Hey, folks!" he called out. His face was kind and weathered, his hair straight and sandy. A couple of young boys' heads popped up and peered out the window.

"Say, Anna, looks like you're in need of a car wash. Want me to send the boys over? We sure love that Bel Air, and hate to see it so dusty." Anna had a racy '55 red Chevy convertible.

"Maybe later," she said. "Say, Joe, this is my niece, Dovey. She's come to spend the summer with me." Anna put her hand on my head. Maybe she was the cuddly type, after all.

"No kidding?" said Joe. "Well, that's swell. You think she'll cotton to life in the boonies?"

They laughed. "Guess she'll just have to, Joe."

"Well, come on over whenever you get the chance. Glad to have you come join us." We nodded. "And feel free to ride ol' Walter if you get the notion."

Joe waved a ruddy hand and the boys grinned gap-toothed smiles. The air was cooling off now as dusk set in. "Goodbye now!" he said.

"They'll be having their big family reunion in Oklahoma in August," said Anna. "I've been before, and it's always a lot of fun. You probably won't see his wife Bernice until then. She's gone down there to take care of her sick mother."

Joe looked like the type of man who would marry

the right woman and stay together forever. I wanted to meet Bernice. Joe seemed as solid and reliable as his sturdy pale blue pickup, with lively eyes to match, content and at peace with his lot in the world.

"That Joe," said Anna. "Why, before I met my honey, I would've gone after Joe in a minute. If he hadn't been married, of course." Her eyes followed his truck down the road and around the bend.

Walter nipped my thumb. "Yeow!" I yelled. I looked to see if the skin had been broken. Anna laughed and turned around to Walter. "Hungry, huh? Well, next time we'll bring more."

Walter put his face close to mine, allowing me to breathe in his warm horsey breath. I stroked his muzzle and patted his coarse mane. It reminded me of the string on my violin bow. I was getting hungry too, and imagined a big plate of mashed potatoes and green beans.

"Well, let's go," said Anna. "I'm starving."

We got back in the car and I held my right arm out the window, pressing against the power of the wind. It was a motion that always irritated my parents, but Anna didn't even seem to notice.

She turned the radio back on. We could still pick up KLWN, though we were far away from its familiar blinking tower. Paul Anka was crooning now. *"Put your head on my shoulder,"* he urged. *"Whisper in my ear, Ba–by,"* Anna sang.

I wished she'd tone it down a little; that song

always made me think of Bobby Birdsong, and the time he asked me to dance with him. He was the only other Indian in my entire class, a Choctaw from Alabama. It was in the spring, our last school dance, and I wasn't sure I would even get picked. It was the final song of the evening, and already half over. Some of the chaperones were starting to look restless.

Then it happened, and suddenly I was in Bobby's arms. He danced closer than I'd expected him to, and we didn't say a word. I tried to calm down and feel what it felt like, but I was too excited. I had adored him the whole semester, but had never gotten past hello.

Soon it was over, and my head was no longer on his shoulder. My body and heart yearned to sway back and forth forever, but the record stopped. Or had it? It had a funny skip at the end, and Paul seemed to be hiccuping the word "*shoul–der*" over and over. I giggled and we slowly pulled apart.

"Thank you, Eleanor," he said sweetly. Though I'd always hated my name, the way he pronounced it made me melt. I was in heaven.

That was the end of the dance, and everyone left the gymnasium to the harsh clapping of Miss Rut-tan, who would have no lingering embraces or smooching. I went outside in the cool air and saw Dad, sitting in the Plymouth and frowning at his watch.

"So — you dating yet?" asked Anna.

I paused a moment. I wasn't sure. The dance wasn't really a date.

"Not really," I said.

"Folks think you're too young?" She smiled.

"They're pretty strict about stuff like that," I said. "They won't even let me shave my legs or wear a bra." I looked down at the dark peach fuzz on my calves.

"Sounds like they don't want you to grow up." I nodded. "And I suppose they would prefer that you not get your periods, either."

We laughed. I was somewhat embarrassed. The girls in our class had been corralled into watching the special film on reproduction, which showed cartoon eggs being fertilized, and the Fallopian tubes and some kinds of islands. It was more like a geography lesson than anything else, and left most of us more confused than before. My friend Sally still swore that a kiss could get you pregnant.

"My parents never told me the facts of life," I said. "They're not the type."

"I know," said Anna. "And those silly little booklets you get in school about hygiene and dating and growing up, they don't tell you what you really want to know."

"Yeah," I said. "But then Evelyn Morris told me the real stuff after school one day. It was too weird to think about. All I think about is kissing and holding hands and stuff." Maybe I was getting too personal.

Anna looked tenderly at me. "Yes, it's those sweet, romantic things we really need. Poems, whispers, smooches, dancing close." She flashed a devilish smile. "Though it sure is fun to be a wild animal, too!"

The brilliance of the day was over. Gray dots covered the fields. Headlights and house lights were blinking on. The weight of my bony bottom pushed uncomfortably against the seat. I closed my eyes and felt a strange peace.

"Not much further, Dove," said Anna. I was drifting off to my favorite dream places. Islands with turquoise seas, lush, wet grasses and palm trees everywhere. I flew like a seagull, soaring above, riding the currents, higher and higher, watching the colors below . . .

· 2 ·

"Wake up, Dovey." I plummeted. "We're here."

"What?" I said groggily. The sun was starting to go down.

"I never knew you snored." Anna nudged me with her elbow and laughed. "Louder even than my ex-husband. Yes, even louder than Gerald." Anna messed up my hair and shook my shoulder.

She got out and started hauling out my suitcase and the groceries. "Come on!" she yelled. "Grab a sack and come on in. I'm starving."

I was, too. I had lost track of time and felt like I was in another country, though the air still smelled sweet with sorghum and wheat. My senses perked up when I caught a whiff of horse, but when I squinted and looked around, I saw nothing.

Anna's house was small, just one bedroom, a kitchen, a tiny bath and a living-dining room. There was going to be even less privacy here than I'd had in

Lawrence. But she had a color TV, which thrilled me, and I shrieked when I saw it. Anna laughed and pointed to the couch, which was made up as a bed. I put my suitcase next to it. The house was tidy and comfortable, and smelled good, like Lux soap.

"Just bring the groceries in the kitchen," Anna's voice said from the depths of the icebox. "You like to cook?"

I did, though I never got a respite at home. Mother was always coming down with something, and Daddy thought that cooking, except for the occasional barbecue, was woman's work.

"Yes," I said. "What sounds good?"

"Anything," said Anna. "You want to start, and I'll take a quick shower?"

"Sure," I said, following her to the icebox. It was a cornucopia of meats, fruits and vegetables, milk, bread, butter, pop, and beer. I'd never seen such wild variety before.

She went into the bathroom and turned on the shower. I pulled out handfuls of this and that, looking for leftovers first. There were potatoes, chicken, barley, fresh spices, and jars of stock. My hands knew what to do, and I set about peeling, chopping, and boiling, enjoying the comfort of familiarity, the excitement of abundance.

I looked at my reflection in the window over the sink. My brown hair was a mass of windblown tan-

gles, and my skin was covered by a thin film of dust.
My eyes looked even larger than usual, and nearly
black, like my father's. He and I were dark-skinned
Chickasaws; Mama's skin was light.

The stew was boiling like a witch's brew. I turned
it down to simmer. Anna seemed to be simmering,
too, in a shower so hot that steam was escaping into
the hallway as the door slowly opened.

"Damned door!" Anna shouted. "Dovey, can you
shut it, please?"

I pushed it shut, but it still wanted to drift. I
found a carton of empty Coke bottles and put it next
to the door. Anna resumed singing, *"She wore blue
vel–vet, whoa, whoa, whoa . . ."*

I smiled and set the table. My fingers opened the
proper cupboards as if I had lived in this house all
my life. In a matter of moments, I had set the table
and folded the napkins into neat triangles. I cleared
off the clutter of Anna's magazines from the table. In
a drawer I found a lovely blue taper, which I carefully placed in the center of things.

"Just a few more minutes, okay, Dove? Gotta
shave these legs."

"Sure," I said, stirring the stew and slicing some
bread.

"I keep these legs as smooth as glass," she said.
"Just in case, you know."

The phone rang and I went into the hallway to get
it. It was a man. His voice sounded tender, like Paul

Anka's, then changed when he realized I wasn't Anna.

"Who is it?" asked Anna. She pushed the door slightly open, giving me a glimpse of her nude profile, with one leg propped up in the lavatory. The pleasant smell of shaving lather greeted me. I tried not to look at her. Nudity was completely taboo in my house.

"Roy somebody," I said, muffling the receiver behind my back.

"Oh, Troy," she said, her voice softening. "Tell him I've got company, and I'll call him back in a minute, okay?"

He'd heard, and said to tell Anna that he'd drop by tomorrow. My mind saw him in an Army uniform, tall and handsome, holding a dazzling engagement ring behind his back. I wondered if Anna dated lots of men, and if she ever wanted to marry again. Two divorces were a lot around here, bordering on the scandalous.

"Got a date with an angel," Anna warbled. Her voice modulated a step up, as though shifting into fourth gear. *"Gonna meet him at seven . . ."*

She rushed from the bathroom into her bedroom, and apologized again. "Just another little minute, Baby," she said. "Then I'll take over."

Nobody had ever called me "Baby" before, and I smiled at the warm feeling it gave me.

I served two bowls of stew and placed bread and

cheese on the salad plates. I sat down and blew steam from my bowl. It looked like the tropical clouds in my dreams, floating wistfully above.

"Oh, my Lord in heavens!" Anna yelled as she waltzed into the room. "You've already done everything!"

I smiled and enjoyed her surprise. Her narrow black eyes widened and her arms opened up to hug me. I loved the clean wet smell of her hair as it rubbed against my cheek and the peck that followed. She wore a soft pale blue chenille bathrobe over her pajamas.

"I'm not used to this kind of treatment," she said. Neither was I, and it felt pretty good.

"Why, I can't remember the last time somebody cooked for me." She leaned forward and inhaled the hearty aroma. "Mmmmmm, you even know how to use spices!"

I nodded and passed her the bread and cheese. She lit the candle and smiled at me as though we shared some special secret, some hidden code or magic remedy.

· 3 ·

The sun woke me up early. I liked sleeping on the couch; it conformed to my angular body and made me feel like the transient that I was. It was also on the other side of the wall from Anna's room, so I could hear her every murmur in the night, her radio playing, the bed groaning whenever she made the slightest shift. One time I heard her talking in her sleep, moaning and calling out someone's name. "Troy," she murmured. She sounded wounded, or ecstatically happy.

I got up and looked in the mirror. There were mirrors all over the place, at least one in each room. I could see myself coming and going, and catch a sideways glance of my profile from the corner of my eye. My face looked back. It was Wednesday's child, as usual — too deep, too serious. My braids were messy. I yanked the rubber bands and let them fall. Instantly the braids were undone; even coated with dust my hair was that slippery.

Then I noticed a new expression, at least one I hadn't seen before. My cheeks were flushed, my lips fuller and brighter. But my body was still straight as a match. I thought of my friend Sharon, who started filling out when she was only ten. She had even gotten her period then! I still didn't feel ready for periods; I reveled in running and horses and hanging upside down from the nearest tree limb.

Anna would be getting up soon. Chores would probably need doing and my quiet time would be broken by a million noises. What time would she leave for work? I knew she was a waitress, but I didn't know where. I looked out the dusty kitchen window as I absent-mindedly scrubbed the sink. There was a whole different rhythm out here in the country — busy, yet peaceful; each person working alone, yet for the good of all. And the fruits of their labor were laid out for the world to see.

Joe on his tractor was a dark speck riding a larger green speck. His rows marched out straight and determined. It was Monday, and I was already starting to feel at home.

Anna's alarm went off, buzzing the whole house. A dog barked outside. "Knock it off, Bosco!" yelled Anna. "I'll feed you in a minute!"

So, we had a dog. That was good. I'd always wanted one. I hoped he was big and goofy, the kind that would jump up and slobber on me. I opened the door a crack and saw the most excited mutt in the world. He was big, and straight out of Disney. He tried to worm his way inside, but I wasn't sure yet what the house rules were.

I washed my hands and looked for some coffee. I knew Anna drank it morning, noon, and night. There was a pound bag of A&P percolator grind on the top shelf. The aroma invigorated me as I stuck my nose in the bag and hummed a commercial jingle. I scooped out a pot's worth and made the percolating noises as I scavenged for bacon, eggs, and grits. In minutes I had two eggs and five strips of bacon frying, and three biscuits in the oven. Mama always liked her eggs just so, but I didn't know about Anna.

"Well, I've died and gone to heaven!" she said, trying to run a brush through her tangled mane.

For the first time, I noticed her strong resemblance to my father. He was an alcoholic, like a lot of Indians we knew, and I wondered if Anna might be, too.

"I *am* leading the pampered life," she said. "You're as hard a worker as I am. Don't have to tell you anything."

I smiled as she hugged me. My body was starting to crave the hugs. Often I would try to hug Mama as she sat in her bed week after week with some new "condition," but all I could feel were her sickness and despair. Anna's hugs were full of energy and life.

"Mind if I eat later?" I said. "I'm not quite hungry yet."

"No problem," said Anna. "I skip breakfast half the time." She filled food and water bowls for Bosco. "He's not really mine, you know. Just appeared on my doorstep a few weeks ago." She opened the door and a pink tongue pushed its way in. "But how could I say no to him?" She laughed and took the food out to the porch.

Bosco whined eagerly as he looked at his food, as though it were some miraculous twice-a-day blessing. "He was skin and bones when he came here."

Anna ate her breakfast. I wondered who was cooking for Mama. Probably Edna, from the church. She had a mission to save lost souls, and was ready to do anything that might hurry it along.

"Well, Dovey," said Anna, wolfing down her eggs, "I've got to go to the truck stop soon. Do you want to go with me?"

So. She worked at Don's Truck Stop. I'd noticed it last night. A little white square of a building surrounded by pickups and cars of all ages.

"Sure," I said.

"My shift is eight hours, so you might want to bring along a book or something."

We cleared off the table and washed the dishes. I picked up a women's magazine from a tall stack and followed Anna out. She hopped in the Chevy and warmed it up, her foot pressing up and down on the gas pedal.

"I love you, a bushel and a peck. You bet your dirty neck, I do," she sang.

I'd never gone to work with anyone before; it sounded exciting.

We followed the roads until we reached the main highway. Joe's place was just on the other side. Not so far at all. He waved from atop his John Deere. At the edge of Joe's property was a lovely round pond. His boys played next to its sparkling green water, watching a paper boat drift slowly from their reach. The truck stop was only another mile and a half more.

I saw the sign coming up. The *D* was flaking off, so it looked more like "on's."

"Well, here we are," said Anna. She pulled around to the back and parked at the end of a row of pickups.

She led me through the back door and past a tiny office. A man sat at the desk, from which a roll of adding machine tape curled to the floor.

"Hi, Anna," he said, looking up as we walked by. Anna took her apron from a hook on the wall and threw it over her head. Her name was embroidered in red cursive over the right breast pocket, next to a faded ketchup stain.

" 'Morning, Don," she said, tying the apron behind her back.

"This must be your niece," said Don, rising and extending a burly hand to me. "Pleased to meet you, Eleanor." His face was round and tan, his bald head sported a handful of gray hairs, and a cigarette dangled from the corner of his mouth.

"Dove," she said, looking at me. "This is Don. I know he looks mean, but he's as sweet as a little pussy cat."

"Oh, yeah?" He laughed. He leaned back and patted his belly. "Don't make me use the whip." He pointed to an ornate bullwhip mounted on the wall over his desk, with a plaque next to it. I squinted to read: "To Don, from the chain gang."

Anna grinned and nudged me down the narrow hallway. On the right was the kitchen. Big beefy smells poured out, making me salivate. A gnarled woman bent over the steaming grill.

"That's Inez," said Anna. "Been here for forty years."

Anna pointed to the corner table. "Sit here," she said, "next to the kitchen. And let me know when you're hungry."

She walked briskly toward the front, surveying the booths and tables that needed cleaning. Her standards were high for a greasy spoon like this. I wondered why she didn't move to Lawrence and work at the fancy Eldridge Hotel. Mama had told me that William Holden had stayed there when they were filming the movie *Picnic*.

I liked the darkness of my corner. From it I could see everything in the large open room. Anna switched on the electric wall hangings that advertised various beers. My favorite was the one with the waterfall. It truly looked like the water was flowing down, down, down into the crystal stream below. An Indian with a feather on his head navigated a birch bark canoe, and the skies were faded blue, with big fluffy clouds. I envied that Indian, and the harmonious life his people lived. Mine seemed lost between past and present, the reservation and the city, pride and shame.

My mother had married the handsomest athlete at Haskell Indian Institute, Louis Derrysaw, a Chickasaw. He was tall and broad, with an easy smile full of perfect white teeth. But now I had to search far back in my memory to find that man. Several teeth were missing and he found little to make him smile. Mama said he felt worthless without a job, and he shunned Mama and me in favor of his liquor. I used to be the apple of his eye; now his eyes were shot with blood, and often cast down.

"Juice?" a voice asked. It was Anna.

"Thank you," I said, trying to smile.

"Listen, hon, if you're bored already, we have a

big bunch of magazines over there." She pointed to a rack by the juke box. "Mostly *Life*." She patted my hair. I smiled and nodded.

People were coming in now. Country folks with hearty appetites. No late sleepers, these. Tending land allowed for little rest; weekends meant little more leisure time than the rest of the week provided.

"Hello, Pat, Vivian," said Anna, seating a large sunburned couple. "You want the usual?"

"You know us, Anna," said Vivian, looking at her husband as she waved away the menus.

"Lester's leg on the mend?" Anna asked. "Heard he broke his leg driving the tractor last week."

"Yeah," said Pat. "Drove it straight into a ditch. I'm gonna be shorthanded this season, maybe hafta borry a neighbor's son for baling."

Vivian shook her head and squeezed Anna's arm. "It's hard, only having one child to help out. I guess I'm barren or something."

Anna shook her head as she poured their coffee into thick round beige mugs. A large convoy of truckers pushed through the front door, laughing and snorting. The morning quiet was over.

"Oh, man, Harry, that was a good 'un! Cain't tell *that* one to the wife!"

Anna assembled them around two tables pushed together in the center of the room. One of the men got up and put some coins in the juke. He danced his way back to the table, twisting his short stocky body and singing along with Bill Haley and the Comets. *"One o'clock, two o'clock, three o'clock rock . . ."*

The noise enveloped and comforted me. I envied large, animated families, and planned to have a house full of children. My house would be happy, loud, and warm. Children would swarm the house like flies, and I would never lay a hand against a one of them. I pulled a napkin from the dispenser and started to name them. The last one, the seventh, was Birdsong.

A plate of bacon, eggs, and grits slid under my nose. Anna smiled. "You hungry yet?"

A moment earlier I would have said no, but the aroma was unbearably enticing. I felt like a queen, being served this way. My parents seldom took me out to eat, and when they did they couldn't truly enjoy it for worrying about the money.

I pierced the yolks and watched them run down the whites and toward the grits like yellow lava. Then I fortified the grits into a wall to spare the bacon. It was crisp and evenly cooked, the way I liked it. I ate the golden yolks first, then the whites, then the grits. Bacon was my favorite, so I saved it for last. I loved its crunch, the strong salty flavor. *It must be what a man's mouth tastes like,* I guessed.

Men kept coming in, and Anna never lost her rhythm or her head. One time the stocky guy, Pete, even whirled her into a jitterbug as she walked past. Her wide hips swiveled sensuously and he pulled her close to him, but the steaming platter of food in her right hand miraculously stayed parallel to the floor. I felt a flush of pride in my connection to this woman.

I walked over to the table of magazines and found a *Seventeen*. The first page was an ad for a roll-on deodorant. My armpits still smelled like a child's, though last week I had noticed a few wisps of thin, dark hair there.

Anna cleared my table and patted my head.

The girl in the ad was pretty. Blonde and curvy. Blue-eyed and coy. Except for the unoffending armpits, she was everything I wasn't. I closed the magazine and looked back at the Indian in the clock. Suddenly sleepy, I put my head on the table and drifted off.

I thought it was the music that woke me up, but the juke box was silent. It must have been his eyes. Sitting alone at the opposite end of the room was a teenage boy with dark, intense eyes. He stared at me without blinking or smiling. Though I tried to look at the rest of him, all I could see were his eyes. It was as though we were locked together in a mysterious dance.

It was only when Don walked in front of me that I realized I wasn't dreaming. "Hungry?" he asked. I looked up at him, confused.

"Uh, no, thanks."

"Well, my little beanpole," he said, bending down, a drop of sweat falling from his brow, "we're going to have to fatten you up this summer."

"Okay," I said, wishing he would move so that I could see the magical boy.

But when Don left to return to the kitchen, the dark eyes were gone. I walked outside and looked around, and saw only dogs and trucks and fields of wheat. The sun was wonderfully hot, and my heart was beating faster than usual. Like a scared rabbit. Except that I wasn't scared.

I followed my nose to the wheat field and ran until it surrounded me. The sweet yellow fragrance enveloped me and the beards softly caressed my body. The dirt was rich, but dry. I dug my hands into it and watched it fall through my open fingers. Someday this will be me, I thought. Something fertile and nourishing that people would give thanks for. I liked the idea. My pulse quieted and I squatted, hugging my knees.

Again, a tiredness came upon me, and I lay down and hummed. In my dreams I searched for the magical eyes.

· 4 ·

A horn blared like an alarm clock. I leaped up. The sun floated in the west. Anna must be worried about me. I dusted myself off and ran back to the restaurant. It was past time for supper.

I opened the door and looked around. Anna's laugh came from the kitchen. I sat down at my table and looked at the menu. My stomach felt hollow and empty.

"Well, there you are!" said Anna, pulling my ear. "Figured you'd show up when you got hungry enough."

I laughed and was glad she was so unconcerned. Mama always made me account for every moment out of her sight.

"You dusty little thing!" she said, touching my long nose. "You look like Bosco, always crawling around under the car and rolling in the dirt. A pig would be a cleaner pet."

My stomach growled. I was hungrier than I'd been in a long time.

"Ready?" said Anna.

"For supper?"

She laughed and shook her head. "To go home."

My face fell. "Oh," I said. I wanted to be served one more time.

"We've got plenty of food at home. You can make up whatever you like."

I put the magazine away and walked down the hallway.

" 'Bye, ladies," said Don, sticking his head out of the office.

"Ta ta," said Anna. I gave a little wave. We got in the car and looked ahead.

"My feet are killing me," said Anna. "I'm going to soak 'em in Epsom salts tonight and just stay off 'em." She smiled slyly. " 'Course, Troy ought to help me there."

Troy. Troy was coming over tonight. I looked at Anna. Her face had brightened. She started the engine.

"I hope you don't mind, Dove," she said.

I shook my head.

"Just don't tell your folks, okay? See, sometimes he spends the night."

"Oh, I wouldn't," I said. In fact, I found the idea of being near such a passionate couple intensely exciting.

In no time we were home. Anna headed straight for the shower, while I made a beeline for the icebox. I pulled out ground hamburger meat and bell peppers. My white grandmother had taught me to stuff and bake bell peppers, which she called "mangoes." Only much later did I discover the splendid tropical fruit that properly claimed the name.

I mixed in onions and spices and slid the peppers in the oven. Next I brewed teabags for iced tea. My stomach begged for more, so I boiled potatoes, squash, rutabaga, and garlic. While everything cooked, I munched on a raw carrot.

What was this? I wondered. A new growth spurt? I hadn't had one in a while. At least I didn't need to worry about getting fat.

Anna sang. *"Wider than a mile. I'm crossing you in style, some day."*

When was Troy coming, anyway?

"Wherever you're flowing, I'm going, your way."

So, what was I supposed to do — disappear?

"Two drifters, off to see the world. There's such a lot of world to see."

I hastily set the table and sat down. My mind shifted back to the boy at Don's. Had anyone else seen him? I decided to ask Anna later.

Bosco was scratching at the door. I went out and poured some food into his bowl. He was ravenous, too. I sat next to him, my back against the warmth of the house, and watched how his mouth and tongue worked to bring the little pellets into his body. The taste buds seemed entirely bypassed. I loved this creature, so free and open and warm.

I had heard that dogs are supposed to usher the dead into the next world. I couldn't think of a more appealing companion than Bosco.

"My huckleberry friend," finished Anna, turning off the shower. *"Moon River."* She pulled open the curtain and tiptoed to her room. *"And me."*

She opened and shut drawers and turned on the stereo. Frank Sinatra started to croon. The sun felt good on my face. Bosco cleaned his bowl and curled up next to my leg. I breathed in deeply and let the peace penetrate my insides.

Outside a car was approaching, pushing the limits of our unpaved road. A cloud of dust whirled nearer, then the car stopped and a man got out. He was Indian, tall and lanky, dressed in khaki and construction boots. I guessed him to be about thirty.

"'Lo," he said, smiling shyly. Bosco roused and licked the man's shoe.

"'Lo, Bosco," he said, grinning.

"I'm Eleanor," I said, rising. "You must be —"

I stopped. Perhaps he was someone else.

"Troy," he said, gripping my hand. "I heard you were visiting your auntie this summer."

I nodded and admired the slant and darkness of

his eyes. He leaned over and whispered softly.

"Now, don't say anything, but just maybe, if the Spirit is good to me, I'll be your uncle someday."

His eyes shone and I felt myself smiling back. My family could surely benefit from one such as this.

"I don't care if Anna is sour on marriage," he said gently. "She is the only one for me. My heart belongs to her."

"Oh, my Lord!" yelled Anna from the kitchen, as she discovered my latest dinner offering. "Lovey, you've done it again!"

Troy patted my head, tiptoed through the door and stepped behind Anna. He held his arms around her waist and kissed her on the neck. I got goose-bumps.

"Troy!" she shouted. "How long have you been here?" She turned and kissed him on the lips.

"Just blew in," he said.

I went inside and stood.

"Met your lovely niece," he said.

Anna smiled. "She's quite a girl, all right. And my, such a cook!"

We filled up our plates from the kitchen and sat down to feast. Troy held out his arms. I put down my fork and looked at Anna. She extended her hands to him and me, and I held out mine. My parents never did this, or even sat at the table much together. We closed our eyes.

"Bless this food, Great Father," said Troy.

"Thank you for bringing us together in love and friendship. And show us the path to walk." He paused and squeezed my hand.

"Amen," said Anna.

"Amen," I said, opening my eyes. It wasn't the Catholic blessing Mama always said, but it made me feel warm inside.

The food was passed around until it was gone. Troy talked of his work in the oil fields of Oklahoma, of the powwow he'd attended last month, of the Snake Dance he performed there, of his desire to go to college.

"Haskell Indian Institute," he said, his face growing stronger.

Anna's face lit up at the prospect of having him so near.

"I want to use my brain as much as my body," he said. "When I'm older, I want my grandchildren to be proud of me. To know the value of a good education."

Anna ate a slice of rutabaga. She already had a son, Harold. He was seventeen and off somewhere in the Merchant Marine. I wondered how she felt about having any more children. After all, she was thirty-three.

"Excuse me," she said, getting up. "I believe we have some ice cream. Don't we, Dovey?"

Troy looked down at his empty plate. Perhaps he had said too much.

"Yes, I think so," I said, starting to get up.

"I'll get it," said Anna. "You just relax."

She cleared the table and set down little bowls full of chocolate swirl.

"Yum," said Troy. "My favorite."

"Mine, too," I said. I loved eating Hershey's syrup straight out of the can.

Troy mixed the colors together and sensuously licked the first spoonful. Anna followed his lead, smiling slyly. Their eyes blazed with something I'd never witnessed before, but which I supposed was the ultimate dessert — feasting upon the one who sets your soul on fire.

· 5 ·

I cleared the table and offered to wash the dishes. But Troy had other ideas. "You go on and relax, watch some TV," he whispered. "Me and Anna might want to play house."

He winked and patted me on the back, then went to the sink and filled it with hot soapy water and a few squeezes of Palmolive. Anna put on her rubber gloves and started scrubbing. Troy did the rinsing and drying. It seemed a comforting ritual for them, something done many times before, in just the same fashion, unlike Mama and Daddy, who usually fought over who would do dishes, or just left them dirty in the sink, where they would crust over and wait for me.

I backed out of the kitchen doorway and watched them from the hallway as they chatted like magpies, and smooched endlessly.

"You're the cream in my coffee," Troy sang into a

salt shaker that now doubled as a microphone. His slim hips swayed, and I thought of Frank Sinatra. Anna looked almost like Ava Gardner as she batted her eyes and kissed him on the lips.

At the end of the song he said, "I'd be lost without you."

"Me too, darlin'," said Anna, looking straight at him as a water glass slowly submerged into the steamy water.

"Every word I say is true, Ain't nobody else but you." He tossed the cotton dishcloth aside and swept Anna off her feet, then kissed her neck as she leaned back like a swan.

I pulled my head farther from the doorway, not wanting to wreck their moment together. Quickly I tiptoed into the living room and turned on the TV. Unlike them, it took forever to warm up.

It must have been a couple of hours later that I realized I'd fallen asleep. Maybe it was the half can of Hamm's beer Anna had given me. *What's My Line?* was signing off, and Arlene Dahl and Bennett Cerf laughed uproariously as they removed their blindfolds and saw the mystery guest, who was still a mystery to me. John Charles Daly chirped a crisp British goodbye, and then it was my usual bedtime. I wasn't sure what to do next.

The house was strangely silent, but when I

strained to hear over the din of the crickets, I made out the voices of Anna and Troy. They were sitting on the front porch step, glued together, looking up at the starry sky, ablaze with planets and constellations the likes of which I'd never seen in town.

"Hey, you guys," I said quietly, opening the door and standing behind their silhouettes. Anna reached out her arm and squeezed my hand. "Say, Anna," I said, "did you see a teenage guy this afternoon at Don's?"

"Sure," she said, "lots of 'em. What did he look like?"

I shuffled my feet and thought. "Well, I guess he was a little older than me, and he had — dark, pretty eyes."

"Lots of us have dark, pretty eyes," said Anna. "Tell me more."

"I can't, really," I said, frustrated. "Well, guess I'll go to bed now."

Troy squeezed my bare ankle with his long fingers, sending a current of warmth up my right leg. "You sure did conk out there for a while," he said. "Dead to the world."

"Even with all our racket," said Anna. "Well, nighty night. We won't be far behind."

What important racket had I missed out on? I realized I wasn't sleepy at all. I went inside and wandered to the kitchen. There was still a fair amount of coffee in the percolator, which was still on and producing what my Uncle Wing called "cowboy coffee." Being out here on the range, it seemed like a suitable drink. I coated my tongue with the bitter, thick brew, another taste of the grown-up world I was entering. I flicked off the light in the living room and pulled on my pajamas. The kitchen light cast a comforting beam on the floor, nearly parallel to me, and I pulled back the cool sheets and lay down. How to divert my mind? Suddenly I thought of the reunion in August. I had never been to a family reunion, and the excitement and anticipation surprised me with their intensity. Perhaps Joe's family was the perfect family, I thought. His wife would be plump and short, with reddish hair like the boys. She and Joe had probably dated in high school, and never suffered with alcohol or sickness of any kind. The boys would grow up to be farmers too, or one a college graduate. The University of Kansas was not so far away. The house would be cozy and unpretentious, tidy and clean as Father John's rectory. Joe would be open in his love and devotion for Bernice. And she would be the same with him. The relatives? Probably mostly farm folk from Eudora, Ottawa, Pottawatomie, Coffeyville. Pale men with red farmer necks fresh from their tractors and plows.

"Oh, sure," said Anna, laughing, locking the front

screen latch. "Bosco thinks he can sneak in without us even noticing."

"'Night, big guy," said Troy. "Go on now."

A couple of moans later, Bosco plopped himself loudly on the porch and sighed. My eyelids fluttered as I pretended to be asleep, and I adjusted my breathing to a convincing rhythm. But inside, I was a reporter excitedly approaching her assignment on the front lines, or the vigilant profiled Indian on the TV screen after the stations had signed off.

My heart beat so rapidly, I wished I hadn't had the coffee. Perhaps this was wrong, this — spying. This eavesdropping. Better to go outside? No, they'd hear me and worry. Plus, Bosco would probably bark. No, I had to stay here. Their lack of privacy was not my fault. Guilt pushed aside, I settled down with my ear to their wall.

The house was dark now. A few drawers opened and shut, a window fan gently whirred. *Enough to mask the noises,* I worried? *Please, God,* I prayed, *do not hide this mystery from me.*

And then the kiss. Softer than a feather. The mattress twanged a greeting, indiscreet and full of feeling. I closed my eyes and imagined what was going on. My friend Gina had read me parts of *Lady Chatterley's Lover* over the phone when her mother was at work, so my knowledge had increased a lot over the past few weeks.

Three dogs barked at the moon far away. I cursed them and the crickets and the sounds in my head. Were they all conspiring against me? Night time was supposed to be quiet, for Pete's sake!

Something was rocking. Like Grandma's ancient rocking chair. They didn't even wait for the — what do you call it? Foreplay! Why, this would be all over and I'd still be wide awake.

But twenty minutes later, the rocking went on. I could tell they were trying to be quiet, to hold tight the reins of a hundred wild horses. I remembered the time I saw horses doing it in Uncle Wing's barn. The men shooed me out, but not before I caught a powerful glimpse.

Now Anna was saying something. Something like, "No. Not this time, love. Don't use it this time. I think I'm really ready."

Troy couldn't believe it, whatever it was, and asked if she was sure, that their fates could be sealed forever.

"Yes," she said. "I'm ready at last."

The rocking shot up to double time, triple time, in a moaning, groaning frenzy that shook me to my bones. Horses stampeded from their room to my couch, and all through my body. I touched myself the way Gina said she liked to, until I was one throbbing nerve ready to explode. I was on a rollercoaster, out of control. A wave of incredible strength swept over me, first where my hand was, then all over in a warm glow. I thought I might be dying, and wanted to scream, but instead sneezed quietly into my pillow.

Troy gasped, and Anna cried. After a long chant of whispered promises, it was done.

· 6 ·

That night, Grandma Winona appeared before me. She was Daddy's mother, and had died suddenly two years ago. My memories of her were mostly of her rocking me and telling magical stories. She hovered over me and told me not to awaken.

"But, Grandma," I protested, "I'm not —"

"Never mind," she said. "I've come to tell you a story."

I watched her shimmery form, and listened as she slowly recounted an old Indian legend. It told of when the stars took root:

On the moon, a Chickasaw tribe lived and hunted. There was a dangerous forest on the narrow ring of the moon whenever it was new. The people were afraid to enter the forest because it was full of evil spirits and no one had ever returned to tell of it.

One day, the daughter of the chief was walking

close to the forest, when she saw a strange light deep within the trees. Unafraid, she entered the woods to discover what made the light. After a while she came to a cave where an old witch woman sat in front of a fire. The maiden had been taught to respect the elders of her people, and so she asked what she could do to help the woman. Knowing that the maiden's heart was pure, the witch took her into the cave and showed her the wonderful paintings on its walls, which told of a beautiful place called Earth. So lovely were the pictures that the chief's daughter wished to go there. The witch woman agreed to show her the way, but warned her that the only path back to the moon would be a dark one called "death."

The witch conjured an eagle, which took the maiden to Earth. There, she met and fell in love with the son of an Indian chief, and soon they were married. But just before the next spring, she had a dream which revealed that she would have to return to the moon. Sorrow filled her husband when she told him of the dream, but she said that soon he would follow her and live forever in the sky with her father's tribe.

The next morning she died, and anguish filled her husband. But when he looked up into the sky that night, he saw her figure in the burial robe in which she had been laid to rest, all glowing with starlight. A shower of little stars fell from her hand toward him. He fell asleep, and when he awoke he saw that morning had not driven all the stars away. By his feet on the grass were hundreds of little pink and white flowers, shaped like stars. He called to the other Indians and showed them the new flowers, these stars that had fallen during the night. Then they all knew that indeed she was waiting for him to follow her.

One day, he was killed in battle and buried beside his wife. Not long after, their graves were covered with the little pink and white star flowers, like a beautiful blanket. Even today, the flowers cover the prairies far and wide.

"So, you see," said Grandma Winona, "though it may seem that your true love eludes you, you will find him, and also the joy that the moon maiden found."

"Tell me another story," I begged. But she smiled and said, "I must leave now. But hold on to love, and never give up, even if your parents fail you. It is seeking you even as you are seeking it. Like a firefly on a warm summer night, it will pop up where you least expect it."

Then she dissolved into the June night.

In the morning, we were all different. Everyone sensed it, but no one spoke of it. The house seemed to contain more than the three of us, a fullness that was both exciting and comforting.

Troy was hugging Anna, which wasn't unusual, but the look on his face was.

"Gonna have to leave for a few weeks," he said, as Anna buried her head in his shoulder. "I can make good money in the oil fields, and then be back here as soon as I can."

"To stay?" I chirped.

Troy smiled.

"In time for Joe's reunion?"

"In time for the reunion," he said, pulling Anna from his shoulder and kissing her lips.

"Oh, Troy," she said, shaking her head. "I'm getting tired of these goodbyes. Can't you find work someplace closer?"

Troy shook his head. "It's just a few hours away, darlin'. And I'll write you every day. I've got big plans, and big plans take money."

I'd never seen Anna look so shaky. "I know you're right, honey, but I just hate to be apart for even —"

He pulled her tight, then lifted her a few inches off the ground. She smiled in spite of herself.

"Give him your blessing," I heard myself say. It was something Grandma Winona frequently demanded. I felt as though I were the adult, and Anna the child. She looked at Troy and nodded.

"That's better," he said, standing tall. "Now Dovey, you take good care of your aunt while I'm gone."

I nodded and smiled as he leaned down and kissed me on the cheek.

They went in Anna's room to pack, and quickly emerged with his one small bag of possessions.

"Goodbye, Troy," I shouted from the front porch. He drove away as quickly as he had arrived. Anna's words had gotten lost in her throat, and she could only blow silent kisses.

She went back in the house and slumped at the table. "Not even time enough for breakfast," she said, looking gloomily at his half-empty coffee cup.

I poured her a fresh cup and rubbed her shoulders. They were hard as iron.

"Guess it's that time of the month, or something," she said, trying to explain her pain away.

"Yeah," I said, pushing deep into the dense, contracted fibers. I had heard of women's emotions getting turned upside down just before the flood, when the sight of a meadowlark on a rain-soaked branch, or an old person with a cane crossing the street, could suddenly make you cry an ocean of hot tears.

But in my heart, I hoped Anna's period was not about to come. Not this month, or the next, or the seven after that. Instead, I prayed for a fertilized egg, for a sperm swimming mightily against all odds, merging with a circle of perfect love.

· 7 ·

It was Saturday, June 15. Mama still hadn't called. Or Daddy. Mama was surely fretting about me now. She said she'd call once or twice, but would have to keep it short due to the long distance. Oh, I was expecting too much again. Mama probably wasn't thinking about me at all. Her medication had put her into a familiar place where I was just a dim memory.

Daddy was probably out with the boys, assuring the bartender that he was still fit to be behind the wheel. Soon he would go home with his friend Wesley and fall asleep on the couch.

Funny, but the way I felt about my parents was a kind of love that kept me a ways apart. I pitied them the way a nurse does her patients: A big part of me kept clear of the sadness. Maybe I was just pushing it all away, but it almost seemed as if they were not my real parents, if I had any at all. In any case, I couldn't blame them for anything.

I had never really gotten to know Anna before this summer, since she spent most of her visits bickering with my father, trying to get him to move back to Oklahoma, where the rest of the family could keep an eye on him, where they'd give him a job on the farm, where his kin could remind him daily of how his father had slowly poisoned himself from the bottle.

"And those cigarettes, Louis!" his mother, Winona, used to rail. "They've got you in their grip! Now I'm not saying a man shouldn't have a smoke now and then, but Louis, you smoke like a house afire!"

My father would clench his fist, then lower it and turn away. Somewhere in the back of his mind he knew that his people used to smoke tobacco, but never became its slave. It was part of a sacred ritual, the weave of a fabric that was now fast unraveling.

But then, looking out the kitchen window as I washed the dishes, a vision came to me. Mama was brushing her long black hair, which cascaded over her pale Irish shoulders, and she looked down at her bare feet. She was younger than I ever saw her, with a light in her eyes, and her body strong and well. The afternoon light sent golden shafts through a shuttered window, and outside Grandma Winona hummed a distant song as she harvested the sweet corn.

Daddy came in through the doorway toward Mama, his eyes clear and flashing, then paused so as not to disturb her private moment. She sensed his presence, but did not turn around, savoring the love that passed silently between them. Her belly, though flat, was six weeks pregnant, and inside, I swam in a sea of love.

The moment was endless, Mother rhythmically stroking her hair, pulling, then letting go, and Daddy there watching like a lion.

The vision helped me to stop worrying about them, and trust in it. For it was the truth about them, I realized, both then and now. The Spirit had surrounded them with light, and would never take it away.

I loved watching Anna's color TV. My parents still had a tiny black and white set. Two years ago, before Mama got so sick, I had spent the night at my friend Marcia's house, and we watched the first color show we'd ever seen. *Walt Disney's Wonderful World of Color,* on NBC. That was 1961, the year of the Cuban missile crisis, when I thought the world was going to end. Instead, there was color, and a little bit of hope.

Anna and I watched TV every night after supper, but only for an hour or two. Some of the shows were stupid, like *The Beverly Hillbillies* and *The Lucy*

Show. Daddy had always hated *Wagon Train* and other westerns because they made Indians look so bad. I had a crush on "Dr. Kildare" and never missed the news with Walter Cronkite. Anna would watch almost anything, and said Dick Van Dyke was the sexiest thing on TV. I couldn't see that at all.

We also played dominoes, crazy eights, the Soupy Sales Game, and the Rocky and Bullwinkle Game. Anna said that she and Troy liked to play Twister, where the players get all tangled up in each other.

She taught me dances, too. The Mashed Potato, the Bristol Stomp, and our favorite, the Twist.

"Can you believe this silly dance was banned in Florida?" she said. We were swiveling to Chubby Checker's 45.

"No way," I said. I thought of how my girlfriends and I would make our Barbie Dolls slow-dance with Ken.

"You bet," she said. "And it was banned by the New York diocese. And in Red China and South Africa. And South Vietnam. Pierre Salinger even had to deny that anyone was doing the Twist at a White House party."

I laughed. "I guess it was new for people to dance apart like that."

"Yeah, Baby. But Chubby himself admitted it. He said it's sex, pure and simple. You're out on the floor, and someone's shaking their body at you. It's pretty powerful."

"I just think it's fun."

"Okay," she said. "So all you're doing is putting out a cigarette with your feet and wiping your bottom with a bath towel."

"To the beat of the music," I said.

Troy did write as he had promised, every day bringing a new declaration of love. Anna brightened, while I struggled with gloominess at being ignored by my parents. Her abundance simply underscored my deprivation.

But I clung to the vision I had had, and tried to keep it fresh in my mind. At night I would light a candle and chant softly as Anna snored, pray to the Great Spirit, then cross myself for the Catholic God I had met at Mass. I wanted to cover all the bases.

July came with a sudden squall and the sounds of threshing machines all around. Rains had been good to the winter wheat, producing one of the best crops in years.

The outdoors had proved a balm for me, blessed relief from the stale smells of Mama's bedroom, and the mentholated steam that saturated the fabric of our house. At last I could breathe, and gather strength from the forces of nature. It was when I went outside, staring at a purple martin or watching clouds, that I felt as if I were going inside myself. Often I disappeared into the landscape, until something clicked in my head, or a bark from Bosco brought me reluctantly back.

"Come on!" Anna was yelling. "Let's go!"

Where? I wondered. It was her day off, Sunday.

"Just a minute!" I said, rising from the grassy area under my favorite big elm behind the house. I could hear the Chevy purring. Then suddenly the engine stopped.

I frowned as I saw Anna get out of the driver's seat and scoot to the right.

"Time you learned," she said as I followed her beckoning hand into the driver's seat. I had never sat behind the wheel before, at least not while the engine was running.

My face lit up like a neon sign. "Shut the door," she said.

"But Anna," I protested weakly, "I won't get my provisional license until I'm fourteen, in two months. So this is breaking the —"

"Law doesn't bother much with these roads out here," she said. "Besides, if they do stop us, I'll just tell them I sprained my ankle." She smiled slyly.

She pulled out a napkin from the glove compartment and drew a capital H on it. "Reverse is up here, first down here, second up here, and third down here." She thought for a moment, then pointed to the horizontal crossbar. "And neutral is this wiggly space in between." She smiled. "See how simple it is?"

I nodded. I had often watched with vicarious pleasure as Daddy smoothly shifted gears, tensing my arms and feet imperceptibly along with him.

"What about the pedals?" I asked.

"Clutch goes down when you shift or come to a stop," she said. "Work it with the gas when you start off. It doesn't take long to get the hang of it."

I nodded.

"And the brake is in between. All your left foot does is push the clutch."

My feet had had practice with pedals when I played the enormous pipe organ at St. John's Catholic Church. The organist had taught me some of the basics in her spare time, and pretty soon I was playing for the six A.M. Mass. My smallest movements on the keys and pedals would send out a wall of glorious sound that shook the rafters, giving me goosebumps.

I rehearsed the precise orchestration of my movements. "Put it in neutral and start her up," said Anna.

I did, and marveled at the power that awaited my direction.

"Put it in first and head off down that dirt road."

She pointed to the fork that went left, away from the main road.

The clutch felt strange, and pulled away from my foot. The car lurched forward. "Dang," I said. "Killed it."

Anna just sat back, relaxed, and looked ahead, as though she had told me everything there was to know.

I adjusted the rearview mirror and tried again. This time it worked. We were chugging down the road at a grand five miles per hour.

"Wow," I said to myself, squeezing the wheel until my knuckles turned white.

"Now listen to the engine," she said. "When it starts to strain, put it in second."

I nodded, and shifted like a pro. The speed seemed much faster than the needle said we were going, and I started to brake.

"Get on up to third now," she said. "We'll never get anywhere at this rate."

I took a deep breath and pressed the gas pedal. I shifted gears, and the car moved from a choppy trot into a smooth gallop, approaching thirty miles an hour. The engine sounded much happier, but I felt like I was going fifty. I kept feeling for the brake.

"Don't ride the brake or the clutch," she cautioned. "Worst thing you can do."

No, I thought, *the worst would be driving into the*

creek ahead of us. The narrow, flimsy wooden bridge laughed at me, and seemed to pinch off the road from two lanes into one. My throat tightened. I was a pilot aiming for the runway.

"Just get in the middle, since there's nobody coming," she said calmly. "That's good."

We shot through the wooden container like a bullet, as Anna glanced over the side and yelled at two fishermen in the creek. "Hey, get a job!" she said with a laugh.

"That was Inez, the cook from work," she said, "and her brother Frank. They're the cutest couple. Lived together forever. Though I think Inez was engaged once, about forty years ago."

I nodded half-heartedly, but my ears were full of the sounds of driving. The wind whipping by, the purr of the motor, the vibrations of the tires, the slight squeak when I pushed the gas. Music to my ears. We wound around curves and pieces of countryside that continually opened up in a sunny embrace. Though it was all completely new, I wasn't lost at all. Landmarks called out to me, and the sun guided me by its position in the sky. Pretty soon I felt as though I had been driving all my life.

"Inez's brother looks like President Kennedy will in about thirty years," she said. "Such a looker. Doesn't make sense to let a man like that go to waste."

I was relaxed enough to hear Anna now. "What's the matter with him?" I asked.

Anna lowered her voice. "Well, I shouldn't say anything, but I hear he's queer."

"Queer?" I said.

"Oh, you know," said Anna. "He falls for men instead of women. Or, he would if he could keep from being found out."

My mind twisted. "I never knew that people could do that!" Maybe she was kidding.

"Really?" she said. "It's not just men. Some women are that way, too." She shook her head and laughed. "You mean you never heard about Tennessee Williams, or Colette, or Walt Whitman?"

Now I was more confused than ever. "But how could they?"

"Oh," she laughed. "Now I've gone and opened a can of worms. Don't worry, you'll hear about all the details later on."

"Yuck," I said, imagining kissing a girl on the lips. "You lie."

"Indian no speak with forked tongue," said Anna. She started humming the theme from *Bonanza*.

My mind shifted to Laura Caldwell, a big-boned Swedish girl in my drama class. She often acted strange in the dressing room, especially the time last year when we were rehearsing for a Thanksgiving play. In the first place, I was in a bad mood about that holiday, the one Grandma Winona used to call "Black Thursday." Laura ignored my frowns, though, as she and her friends donned their cheap hats and pieces of cardboard with painted-on buckles that covered their sneakers. They were the Pilgrims. I, of course, had to play an Indian, along with two black girls and a Mexican boy.

It was embarrassing enough being in a room full of half-naked girls with better figures than mine. But Laura kept staring at me, displaying her enormous boobs, even when I had nothing on but my panties. Her blue eyes batted affectionately, and when no one else was looking, her lips mouthed a silent "I love you."

I wheeled around and faced the wall, but could still feel her eyes adoring my skinny backside. No girl had ever looked at me with those eyes, and I didn't know what to do.

"Slow up, now," said Anna, bringing me back from my reverie. Horrified, I saw we were going forty-five, much too fast for this stretch of road.

"Just brake real easy now, and pull over," she said, smoothing down her hair. "I'll take us back."

I slowed down to a jerky stop, and put on the parking brake.

"Whew!" I said, sitting back and smiling at Anna. "That was the most fun I've ever had!"

Anna laughed. "You did good, Dovey. I'm proud of you." She smiled and patted my knee. "Why, you'll be a pro by the time you go back home."

We switched places, and I thought of what a wonderful day this was, a day not yet half over, but full of the juices of life. With Anna, it was all juice, and whether sweet or bitter, to be relished.

· 8 ·

It was Thursday, the Fourth of July. Don had decided to give all his employees the day off with pay. I was feeling tired that day and welcomed the chance to do nothing. I lay on the cool pink linoleum floor, my head resting on a round pillow. Anna was on the couch, reading the July 5 issue of *Life*. She had been fighting nausea off and on, and mood swings that caught her off guard. The frequent noise of firecrackers bugged us both.

"Look, Dove," said Anna. "Feel free to go to the fireworks display tonight if you want. There's a pretty good one in Garnett, just down the road. Joe or Inez would be happy to take you. I'm just not up to it today."

"No, thanks," I said. "That's okay."

"You're too old for sparklers and snakes and all that stuff?"

"I guess," I said. "We used to go to the big fireworks show in Lawrence, and it was great." I thought of the heart-stopping pink-and-gold explosions overhead in the velvety sky. The crowd sighing "ooh" and "ahhh." The world seemed to burst with possibilities. "But the last two years, Mama hasn't gone out much, so —"

"So what did you used to do before then?" asked Anna.

"Oh, we'd get together with Grandma Winona and whoever else was around — Uncle Wing sometimes — and drink pop and eat hot dogs and corn on the cob all day. And when I was little, Daddy used to take me to the ice house to get a big block of ice to keep everything cold."

"Ah yes," said Anna. "I do love summer."

The cover of her magazine was about the new Pope. I thought he didn't look as friendly as the one who had just died. Anna said, "I bet this one won't be as open-minded as the last one. It must be hard being a Catholic. Birth control is a big sin, and divorced people like me can't take communion if they get married again." She flipped a few pages.

"Look at this," she said. "Beer cans will never be the same again. The top has a built-in can opener."

"Neat," I said. She put the magazine on the floor so that we both could see, and flipped through it.

"Here's that Ford Econoline van that Joe wants to get," she said. "Only two point seven cents per mile."

I stopped when she got to the story about the Kennedy relatives that JFK was visiting in Ireland. They were not fancy-looking at all, and reminded me of some of the farmers who ate at Don's.

"Look at Josie Ryan," said Anna. "She looks just like the Washington Kennedys."

It was true. JFK was mobbed by excited crowds everywhere he went in Europe. One woman had fainted and was carried away. Just today, we had heard on the radio that JFK and Khrushchev had talked on the phone, saying they both wanted world peace to continue.

Peace, I thought. *Yes.* I closed my eyes and watched as a peaceful moment sprang to mind. It was of Mama and me, three or four years ago. It was a hot summer Saturday, and the noon sun beat mercilessly down on us as we lay in our lounge chairs side by side. Mama was slathered with Coppertone dark tanning lotion, and determined to get a tan. We would do each other's backs, and flip over at the same time. Our portable radio blasted the Top 40 hits, and Mama would sing along with all of them. Sometimes it was so hot that I could feel my heart beating way too fast, but it didn't bother me. I loved the penetrating heat, and just being next to Mama.

Of course, her Irish skin would only turn pink, never tan, while mine bronzed effortlessly.

My mind shifted to Daddy. I hoped he was finding a job. Maybe right now someone was shaking his hand and saying, "Okay, Mr. Derrysaw, you're hired. Can you start tomorrow?"

Anna shut the magazine and lay back, her elbows folded behind her head.

"Anna," I asked, "what jobs did Daddy used to have?"

"Oh," she laughed, "mostly jobs that didn't suit him at all.

"Louis tried to be a salesman, you remember. But he hated twisting people's arms," said Anna. "It wasn't his style. Why, the only time he made money was when he sold fallout shelters!"

We laughed.

"Two years ago," I said, "we all thought the world was going to end. It seemed like the teachers were always telling us to duck under our desks. Like that would help anything."

"There's nothing funny about the end of the world," she said, "but you can only take so much."

"Daddy said his company sold a thousand shelters a week. Or Khrushchev sold them for him, every time he opened his mouth."

"It was true. Lots of my neighbors had them installed, and threatened to gun down anyone to protect their shelters. Old Mr. Everett was real secretive about it. Said he was just repairing some plumbing in his yard. Ha!"

"And remember how Millie's Dress Shoppe sold

'shelterwear'? They even had a dress with a cape that could double as a blanket. Mama got one for a birthday present."

"Yes," said Anna. "Unfortunately, I do."

"And that creepy salesman guy that told Daddy not to worry that the shelters might not work. He said, 'Well, at least the customers couldn't complain.' "

"Louis knew it was crazy, but he made good money back then, and that's when he bought that Corvair. He was so proud of it. Of course, it turned out to be a bomb itself. Why, it hardly ever started." Anna shook her head.

"So it's the perfect economy car." I laughed.

"Louis always did try, but he just couldn't find his place. He was quite an athlete at college, but after that he had to find something that could support his family. Remember, by then your mother was already a teenage mother. And she didn't have a high school diploma.

"She helped out, though. She worked at Burger King, and the Varsity Theatre. Until a couple years ago, she wasn't doing so bad. Your mother is a wonderful woman, Dove. Why, when I first met her, she was hoping to get a job singing."

"Singing?" I asked. I had often heard Mama sing when I was younger, but had never thought much about it. I supposed all mothers sang a lot.

"She had a big strong voice," said Anna, "like that girl in the Ronettes who sings 'Be My Baby.' She could have had a career, I swear, if it hadn't been for her miserable parents, who said it wasn't godly for a woman to perform."

"Why not?"

"They were just impossible," said Anna. "Squashed every dream your mama had."

"I never knew them," I said. "They died a long time ago."

"Listen, Lovey, I don't often speak ill of folks, but I know too much about the Arnolds to be impartial. I'm sure they had their good side, but I know I never saw it. And I swear, I looked hard for it."

"Mama never talks about them. When I used to ask, she just said there wasn't much to say. She said her father took odd jobs, and her mom always stayed at home."

"With the kids," said Anna.

"Kids?" I asked. "Mama always said she was an only child."

"I've said too much," said Anna. "You're not supposed to know."

I pulled on Anna's arm. "Please. I'll never let on. Never in a million years. I'm famous at school for not telling secrets."

Anna looked off and bit her lip. Her eyes were moist. We sat in silence. Then she got up and pulled her Bible from the shelf. "Swear on it," she said solemnly.

"I swear." I put my hand on it the way I had seen people do on *Perry Mason*. *Cross my heart and hope to die,* I thought. *Stick a needle in my eye.*

She looked at me. "Let's just say that your mother had twin sisters once upon a time."

"She did?" I asked. "Older or younger?" I wondered what they looked like.

"Older. They were born in nineteen-thirty. Before they turned two, they both drowned. Under mysterious circumstances. No charges were ever filed."

"God," I said, my head spinning. "You don't mean that they were —"

"I don't mean anything. But there was a lot of talk around town. And there are other things that went beyond just gossip. Like the beatings they gave your mother, and the time they shot her pet dog when he wet their sofa, and — that's all I'll say. And if you ever so much as breathe a word of this —"

"I promise, Anna. I swear." I looked in her eyes and felt as if my head were coming off.

"I know your mama tries your patience, Dove, but she doesn't mean to. Let's pray that she will find her way out."

We closed our eyes and squeezed hands. I squinted and clenched my teeth. When I was finished, my face was completely wet.

· 9 ·

It was Friday, July 12, two days before Mama's birthday, and I decided to stay home for a change instead of going to work with Anna. I opened my writing tablet and began to write.

Dear Mama,

I hope this letter gets to you on the 14th, and that you have a very happy birthday. And if you start to worry, just think — you're not even thirty yet!

I have been as good about writing as you and Daddy have. I guess we are not the best at that kind of thing. But I have been thinking of you every day and hope that things are going better. Has Daddy come home yet? Did he get a job?

Aunt Anna is taking good care of me. I hope the church ladies are taking care of you. Be sure and take your medicine at the right times.

Don't worry about anything. The Blessed
Virgin is smiling down at you.
  Love always,
  Eleanor

I wasn't sure about the Blessed Virgin part, but
Mama was stubborn in her beliefs, and warned
Daddy that the Indians wouldn't be able to go to
heaven if they didn't accept Jesus.

"Oh, so you whites have taken that away from us,
too?" he chided.

Daddy tried going to Mass with Mama, back
when I was little, but he was confused by the Latin,
the genuflecting and crossing, and the apparent lack
of emotion. But when he was sober, he remembered
the Indian ways, and found his own peace.

I walked the line of red bricks that outlined the
driveway, put the letter in the silver mailbox, held
up miraculously by a stiff silver chain, and pulled up
the red flag.

Bosco followed me to the house and flopped on
the porch. I sat next to him and let him nuzzle my
neck.

"You're the best dog in the world," I said. "And
I'd take you back to Lawrence with me, if I could."

Something in me broke loose, like a bag of waters,
and I found myself crying for the next two hours. It
was the first time in many years. I watched images fly

past, none lingering long. There was Mama curled up like a worm in the bed, freezing during the dog days of August. Daddy walking out the door at midnight, holding a bottle in a paper bag by the neck. Grandma Winona, telling me about the Chickasaw Trail of Tears in 1837, and the long, sadly moving column of Indians leaving their sacred homeland. A statue of the Sacred Heart of Mary in St. John's Church. Julius LaRosa singing a sappy song on *The Arthur Godfrey Show*. The inauguration of President Kennedy. Bobby Birdsong holding me in his arms. Cowboy movies where the audience clapped every time an Indian was killed. Our astronauts waving to the world before they blasted off into space. The U.S. flag.

I followed my trail of tears, enjoying the long-denied release. My lungs expanded, a weight fell away. Bosco licked my tears and kept a paw on my leg.

I was empty the rest of the day, not productive as usual, but slow as molasses, and wide open. Anna would be surprised that I hadn't washed a single dish, swept a single cobweb, uttered a single word.

When she got home, I simply opened the door and put my arms around her.

For the next two weeks Anna threw up every morning. She tried to keep it quiet, but it was no use. The rest of the day her stomach settled, but then she developed the habit of falling asleep. She was apt to do it anywhere, anytime.

Once Joe had to bring her home from work, she had it so bad.

"Don caught her sleepwalking," he said, chuckling as he led her to her room. "Guess she must have some kind of bug."

"Mmmmmm," I said. But I knew it was the love bug that had caught Anna. She'd stopped drinking coffee and beer, and couldn't stand the sight of eggs. What she wanted morning and night were saltines and hamhocks. She seemed distracted, like she was listening to spirits. When she drove, she piddled along like my grandfather, forcing cars to honk and pass her by. She would simply wave like Miss America, looking slightly tipsy, and continue at her snail's pace. More and more, I was the one who drove.

In the evenings I would rub her feet. Within two minutes she would be asleep on the couch, and unable to rouse for the short stumble to her bed. So I gave up and took to sleeping in her bed, enjoying its expanse and feel, but still listening for any sounds from the other side of the wall.

· 10 ·

Anna's room began revealing itself to me, in bits and pieces. Little was hidden away. Her things were strewn in clumps and piles, covering the table, dresser, and the floor itself. I was timid at first, but soon entered into the mystery of this puzzle, hoping to find pieces of my own world in Anna's.

The books on Chickasaws called to me first, especially the photos. A Chickasaw council from the 1880s. A Chickasaw boarding school in Sulfur, Indian Territory. I stared at these tall, well-proportioned people with reddish-brown skin, big dark eyes, and jet black hair. An air of independence and superiority shone from their faces. The warriors would shave the sides of their heads, leaving a crest on top, while women and older men wore their hair long. One woman, Shunahoyah, or Roaming Woman, dressed in an elegant white blouse and wearing small round earrings, looked back at me with almost the face of Grandma Winona. Was she a relative?

Next I found the letters. The one on top was the most recent and, like all the ones below, was from Grandma Winona. I carefully opened it, my fingers trembling.

Dear Anna,

Old age has seeped into my bones, and I feel the end coming soon.

There is so much I want to tell you, and your brother, the father of my dear Dovey. But the problems with alcohol and the modern way of living apart keep us all unconnected. My heart aches because of that. There is so much to pass on.

We come from a great nation, the Chickasaw Nation. A nation of strong warriors and a people in harmony with all of nature. We came from Mississippi, Alabama, Kentucky, and Tennessee, and were close to our Choctaw brothers and sisters. We had strength and endurance, and could run like the wind. In the thick forests of Tombigbee we made river boats from large logs hollowed by fire, scraped with clam shells. From pines we framed our houses, and with the pitch of pines we made torches to light up the night. My Mama used to make mortar and pestle sets for grinding grain from our beloved red hickory.

Some of this you may know, and some you may not.

We turned eagle feathers into a warrior's mantle, and walnut hulls into a rich dark dye to mix with bear grease for our hair. Even the white men commented on our cleanliness and beauty.

I turned to the next page, but it had coffee stains on it, and all the ink had smeared. I started to cry, then made myself remember this story Grandma used to tell us. I was ten again, and sitting next to her as she knitted blue socks for me.

"My grandfather could catch fish with his hands, and we always had plenty of catfish, suckers, bass, and perch. Mama and I would gather wild onions, grapes, persimmons, plums, blackberries, chestnuts, acorns, and hickory nuts. She pressed dried persimmons into bricks and cakes, and boiled sassafras into a wonderful tea. How I loved the taste of sassafras tea!"

I loved it, too, and the way the flavor always surprised my tongue.

"One day we built, daubed with mortar and dried grass, and completely finished a nice house, whitewashed inside and out. People helped each other back then."

I liked the idea of a house that smelled like grass. "And what about church, Grandma?" I asked. "Did you go to Mass?" I worried about her soul not being saved.

She laughed and shook her head. "Our Supreme Being was Ababinili, who was all of the things above us. We had many gods that helped us and told us where to migrate. They gave us our ceremonies and rituals. We had holy men, the Hopaye, and healers, the Aliktee, who drove away the animal spirits that caused disease, and passed them on to other animals. And everyone knew how to doctor themselves. Our home remedies and herbs worked better than most medicines today."

Grandma Winona took pride that she had never gone to a white doctor. Even a week before she died, when Mama and Daddy had Doctor Johnson come to the house because of her chest pains, she refused to let him touch her. "I have my own medicines," she whispered. "And perhaps, it's time to die."

She told me about our warriors. "They were the fiercest, little Dovey. Never forget that. Over and over they crushed other armies, even the French that tried to force us to serve their nation."

The last page was not so smeared, but it was hard to make out.

So how was it that in less than fifty years we declined so? Well, the elder generation became enraptured by the white man's ways and things,

*and did not transmit our values. And this broke
the chain, and our legacy of pride, and everything
began breaking down. Our proud and unconquered
people became easy marks. We died a bit at a
time. Our wisdom life fell away, and by this
century, hardly any of the young people knew
anything about it, and even the older ones were
starting to forget.*

*Yes, I am old, and often forget where I put my
eyeglasses. But I will never forget where I come
from. Louis, your brother and Dovey's father,
remembers too, when he stops drinking. Dovey
deserves his wisdom, not his trembling hands and
vomit. Do all that you can, Anna, to remember
and then to pass it on.*

*My prayers are with you, and, in these last
days, I search for the means to recover the mighty
warrior power and eternal solace that only
Ababinili can provide.*

Your loving mother,
Winona

Tears ran down my face, and I quickly wiped them
away. Outside my window, an August moon was
rising over the crest of Joe's barn.

· 11 ·

The phone awakened me. I thought it was part of my dream until Anna came in, looking disturbed. She sat on my bed and stroked my foot. "That was your mother," she said.

I sat up on my elbows. "Mama? Can I talk to her?"

Anna shook her head. "No, she just wanted to tell us that she's going away for a while. Doesn't know where."

"What?" I said. "Is she coming back before school starts?"

"Yes," said Anna. "That's all I know. She just said not to worry, but that she's very mixed up and has to get away to sort things out."

"Is she going alone?" I asked.

"She didn't say, Dovey. I don't know what to make of it."

I could imagine Mama standing dazed in the

Greyhound station, wearing her pajamas, buying a ticket to nowhere. Or she might be a shimmery spirit that no one else could even see, unable to put her feet on the ground. What if she forgot her name, and where she came from?

A croaking noise came from my throat, and I tried not to cry. Anna held me close, and helped the tears come out. "Sometimes we have to let people go, even when it hurts," she said.

I buried my head in her chest.

"We all have to find our own way, Dovey," she said. "No one can shield us forever. Let's just pray that the Spirit guides her, and hold her high in our thoughts."

I nodded, and tried to trust in the universe. No, I would not give in to worry.

· 12 ·

"Anna," I said. "Do you know about vision quests?"

"A little," she said. She was wearing work jeans and silver snakeskin cowboy boots. "When I lived in Wisconsin, near the Great Lakes, some of the tribes had them." She was reading a magazine.

"What did they do?"

"It was something that the Ojibway boys did, and they didn't talk about it much to others. They'd go off into the wilderness for four days. But it wasn't the usual Boy Scouts campout, because they'd go one at a time."

"Could you do it on the prairie?" I asked.

Anna looked up from her magazine. I hoped she hadn't seen the article about Jackie Kennedy losing her two-day-old son from hyaline membrane disease. It would just make her worry. "Well, I suppose you could do it anywhere, as long as you're away from folks," she said. "And color TV."

I laughed, and went back to dusting the venetian blinds. It was a mindless chore that never got done if I didn't do it.

"And when the boys came back," said Anna, "the girls noticed something in their eyes, in the way they walked. They had survived without food or water or shelter or anyone to help them out, and it usually showed. They were more men than before."

"What if they got sick?" I asked. "Or bitten by a snake?"

"They had to deal with it. Why, I heard of one boy, William Maytubby, who fell and cracked his skull open. He died. But that was rare. Most boys learned to become friends with animals and the forces of nature, and to watch their step."

I sneezed from all the dust particles in the air.

"Bless you," said Anna.

"Did your son Harold have one?"

"Harold? No, Chickasaws don't have vision quests. And boys aren't doing it much anymore. They just join the Scouts and have a good, safe time. And mothers don't have to worry anymore."

"Well, I dreamed about Grandma Winona last night. She told me I have to find myself. So I think I should go on a vision quest. As soon as possible."

Anna frowned and put down her magazine. "Oh, you do, do you?"

"Yes. I can't remember the whole dream, but I

think I should go for at least two days to fast and pray. To think about life, or ask for a vision. Grandma Winona said not to leave until I had received a gift."

Anna leaned forward in her chair. "Dovey, I try to listen to dreams, too. And sometimes Winona tells me things like she did before she passed on. Like warning me against speeding, or telling me what foods to eat when I get sick. Sometimes she tells me the most amazing things even about the future."

I sat on the sofa across from her. She went on. "But this summer, I'm the one responsible for your safety. I can't just let you go off to God knows where, and not be there if you need me."

"But I'm sure I'll be all right. Please let me. I'm young and strong, and hardly ever careless about things."

Anna looked off. "You dusted those blinds real good."

I clasped my hands together and sat in silence. Silence was my friend, but it often made Anna nervous. I determined not to be the one to break it.

"A lot can happen in two days," she said.

I nodded.

"Of course, I guess you want something to happen. And it's not that I don't trust you, you understand. It's just that I'm the one responsible right now. Of course, God is responsible ultimately. And out here isn't exactly a no man's land. Although, nature is nature. Prairies catch fire, tornadoes and floods come out of nowhere. There are poisonous plants and animals. And being without water is hard on the body, no matter how you look at it." She shook her head and looked off at the prairie that stretched out toward the horizon.

"And what if your folks call and want to talk to you? What do I tell them — lies? Surely you see what a position this puts me in."

I nodded and watched her fingers fidget in her lap, smooth back her hair, and thump rhythmically on the heel of her boot. "Of course, they're not likely to call, the buggers, but if they did —"

She crossed and uncrossed her legs, then got up and paced the room. "This isn't the city, you know. If you get scared, you can't just walk to a phone and call me to come get you." She stopped pacing and looked at me. "And part of it, I know, is just me. Me missing Troy. I get tired of being alone. Why, having you here this summer is as good for me as it is for you."

My heart swelled with love and respect for Anna, and I would not fight her on this.

Finally she went back to the window, raised the blinds and looked out. I could see one cloud, wispy, in the shape of a goose. "Oh, damn," she said quietly, "I guess you can go."

I leaped to my feet and put my arms around her

from behind. We gazed out the window together.

"But just for two days," she said. "On the weekend, when I'll be so busy at Don's that I won't have any time to worry."

"Okay," I said. "I'll leave Friday night and come back Sunday night. And I won't need to go very far out here, to get away from people."

She turned and looked at me, stroking my hair. "And color TV," she said. "That's probably harder for you kids to go without than food, right?"

The phone rang, and she walked off slowly to get it. "Oh, Lord, Lord," she moaned. "What have I gotten myself into?" She picked up the receiver and crossed herself, something I hadn't seen her do in years. But it reminded me of Mama, who had taken to crossing herself every time the phone rang or there was a knock at the door. As though demons were waiting for her at every turn.

Mama, I thought, *be strong. And whatever strength I find, I'll share with you.*

· 13 ·

Two days later it was Friday already, and I could tell Anna wished she could back out of her agreement. But she wasn't that kind. I had had several moments myself when I wished I had forgotten Grandma Winona's dream. After all, what did I know about survival?

The afternoon was dry and sunny, as I looked through my few possessions, deciding what to take. My eyes settled on the dyed pink rabbit's foot that Uncle Wing gave me when I was in the first grade. It would bring good luck, and give me something to hold on to at night.

"Hold still," said Anna, brushing my hair back in a pony tail. "Your hair is getting long now, and you don't want it getting in your way. You'll have plenty more important things to think about." Her eyes were getting wet.

We had just had a late afternoon supper that she

insisted on fixing for me. It had plenty of fat in it, and meat, and things that take a long time to digest, like cashews. All I had really wanted was a Swanson turkey TV dinner. I finally had to push away my plate and refuse any more.

She had insisted also that I wear long pants, an undershirt, a plaid flannel shirt, and a sweater, as well as cowboy boots and a Kansas City A's baseball cap. It seemed too much for summer, but I didn't protest.

"Okay," I said. "Guess I'll go say goodbye to Bosco." But he was way across the road, running west toward Joe's, in the opposite direction from where I would be going.

"What else?" said Anna, her eyes scanning the room for anything that might be of use.

"I don't think you're supposed to take much of anything, are you? That's the whole point."

"I know, I know," she said. "Not even a pocket knife or anything."

I nodded. "So," I said. "I guess I'll be off. And I'll be back before you know it."

She hugged me hard and wouldn't let go.

"Now, don't worry," I said. "Everything will be all right."

"I know, I know."

We walked to the back door and out into the yard. There would be cornfields to walk through, and milo, and soybeans. And somewhere out there, I would find a secluded place just for me.

"Oh, Dove," she said, as I walked off. She waved wildly.

I waved back and smiled, tipping my cap to her. I felt stupid wearing that cap, and planned to take it off as soon as I got out of sight.

I took quick, bold strides to impress her with my confidence, and turned around after twenty minutes to look back. She was still standing on the back porch, waving to the speck that I must have now become. The next time I looked back, the scene had changed completely.

I took off my cap, then realized how hot the sun was, even at five-thirty, and put it back on.

The exercise felt good, and I liked the feeling of the muscles in my legs working hard. I thought of how my history teacher had reminded us once that for most of human history, people had had to walk anywhere they wanted to go.

The days were long, and it seemed earlier than it really was. It was nice not having a clock to look at. The world seemed more open and free.

Just as I stopped paying attention, my right foot sank into a hole and I twisted my ankle. I cried out in pain. My march turned into a hobble.

When dusk started to fall, I began looking for someplace to spend the night. It was hard to know what to look for when I had never camped out a night in my life. Although I wasn't sure where I was, I knew I had been walking due east, for about four miles. I was at the edge of a cornfield and near a narrow creek. Overhead were tall trees whose branches were making lacy silhouettes as night fell. In my mind I heard Grandma Winona whisper, "This is the place."

There really was nothing to do. I realized how much of my time was ordinarily taken up by food — buying it, taking it home, washing it, slicing it, cooking it, cleaning up afterward. Every day, over and over.

I rinsed my hands and face in the shallow creek, and soaked my sore ankle to keep it from swelling. The urge to drink was overpowering, but I fought it off. I didn't know whether it was okay to drink water on a quest, but thought maybe I should play it safe. "Not until Sunday night," I said to my parched throat and insides. "I can do this."

The cool air eased the thirst a little, and I lay back against a tree. What kind was it? "Nice tree," I said, laughing. I patted its rough bark. Overhead, through the branches, I saw a nearly full moon rising in the east. Though I knew I was not so far from Anna, I felt disconnected, and the feeling grew as the minutes went by. Or were they half-hours, or hours? It was getting hard to tell. I felt more alone than I had ever felt before, and the strange noises from the grasses and the trees and the water made me feel worse. What was I doing here? Just wallowing in pain? I forced myself to close my eyes and go to sleep.

No sooner had I drifted off than I was awakened by a giant thunderclap so loud it made my ears ring. My eyes popped open and I saw a jagged bolt of lightning that looked dangerously near. I counted, "One thousand one, one thousand two, one thousand —" Again, a deafening peal of thunder. The lightning was only about half a mile away. Rain fell in sheets, and though I wanted to stay dry under the tree, I knew it was the worst place to be.

I ran out into the cornfield and looked around. In no time I was drenched. What had Daddy told me when I was little? Something about making yourself small, not a target. Something about dropping to the ground, or crouching, if you felt your hair start to stand on edge. I fell through tall corn to the mud below, and felt in my pocket for my rabbit's foot. I pushed on it as hard as I could, as if to release magical powers.

God, I thought, *please don't let me die out here. Please.*

This safety position turned out to be a natural praying position, and I prayed first to the Catholic God, then the Chickasaw god, then Lady Luck herself. I called on the wisdom of Grandma Winona, and Daddy and Anna, and everything I'd ever learned in school. I cradled my soft belly, and thanked my insides for all they'd done for me, though I seldom thought of them — my heart, still beating; my lungs, still sucking in air. The thunder and lightning doubled in intensity, set fire to a nearby tree, then, just as quickly, the rain put the fire out.

I wondered who would find my body if I didn't survive. Some poor unsuspecting farmer, out mending his fences? And would he see me first, or smell me? I wondered what a rotting person smelled like. Would the vultures come swiftly and leave only my bones? How would Anna ever get over it? Or Mama, and Daddy? God, I could wreck everything by being in the wrong place now.

But Grandma Winona had told me this was the right place, and I had to trust her. Unless, of course, she just missed me so much that she wanted me up in heaven with her. But she didn't believe in the kind of Catholic heaven I had learned about. So my death would be a total waste.

I started crying into the mud and rain. I was so little here, so confused and powerless. I heaved and groaned until I sounded like a cow giving birth, and the longer I thought about that, the funnier it seemed. I started laughing.

I leaped to my feet and saw the storm had passed to the south. Already, most of the sky was clear, with stars coming out, and it was as if the storm had never happened. Realizing that I couldn't dry my clothes until tomorrow, I wrung them out and hung them from a low branch. I lay on the soggy bank and quickly fell into a shallow sleep.

When I awoke it was still dark. Completely disoriented, I shouted loud to wake myself up, as I would in a nightmare. But I was already awake. I shivered from the cool creek air. "God," I said, "please don't give me pneumonia." My voice sounded odd to me. It seemed I hadn't spoken in ages, or heard another human voice for as long.

The smell of the wet corn around me reminded me of the stories Grandma Winona used to tell me about the Green Corn Celebration in July, of the games and dances. How the tribes were not allowed to feast on the fresh corn until after the ceremony.

This is hard, I thought, *having food and water around you, and not being able to have any.* Food and water were all I could think about, and my body and mind fought over and over. No wonder quests were often held in the desert!

A big orange ball rose in the east, just after the white ball of the moon had set in the west. *Like counterweights,* I thought. There seemed to be order in the universe; if only I could march in tune with it. I welcomed daybreak and how it got rid of the spooky night feelings. I felt like myself again, and ready to go on.

With my ankle still sore, I would have to keep my physical exercise to a minimum, and concentrate on praying and listening. I would stay in this place, out of sight of everyone, until tomorrow evening. Whatever was to be revealed to me, if anything, would have to happen here.

To the north I saw a line of Canada geese flying in a wobbly V formation. They honked and flapped their wings in a wonderful show of instinct and determination.

I thought about Anna. Was she watching Saturday morning cartoons? Or had she already gone to work? It would be hard for her not to be able to tell anyone what she had let me do. They would tell her it was crazy or something. I tried to imagine her busy at work, waiting endless tables, with hardly a break. And then a letter from Troy waiting for her at the end of the day.

Katydids rasped sweetly, and I hummed along. Thank God they had gotten "Where the Boys Are" out of my head. Connie Francis's melancholy voice had been pestering me for days.

A tree squirrel screeched from over my head, and went flying from a branch. A piece cracked off and scratched me on the arm, stopping short of drawing blood.

I hobbled just a few yards in every direction, and

was amazed at the life around me. I saw hawks, a prairie chicken, a meadowlark, and some jays. Mostly, though, I saw things I didn't know the names of. And I vowed to learn as many as I could when I returned from this journey.

I looked at my feet. They were starting to grow blisters. At least my ankle was not too bad. I put my feet in the clear, shallow, moving water, and was glad I wasn't in the desert.

The whole day I sat and watched the world around me. Memories and worries hit me left and right, but I kept humming with the katydids and didn't get depressed. After several hours I had the odd, almost scary sensation that I didn't exist apart from the world around me. The animals, the sky, the wind in the cottonwoods.

Cottonwood! That was the name of this tree. It had come to me somehow. I put my arms around it and could almost feel the juices circulating inside. It seemed conscious and wise, and I sat beneath it the rest of the day, watching as leaves fell here and there. I liked their valentine shapes.

My insides railed off and on from thirst. I rubbed my belly and whispered, "Tomorrow, tomorrow. I promise." And the thirst would go away for a while.

I drew pictures in the dirt with a stick, then cast leaves out on the water and watched them float out of sight. It was good being out of the harsh summer heat. In the late afternoon a baby garter snake crept toward me. I let him crawl near my leg, then lifted him gently and looked into his round eyes. He seemed to be saying something, but I didn't know what.

Again the air cooled and I faced another night alone. This time I wasn't quite so scared, but I still felt uneasy and vulnerable. At least I had the light of the full moon to comfort me, to give me landmarks. I wasn't sure I could have stood being plunged into darkness all night.

Off in the distance a dog yipped. Or maybe it was a coyote. Time dropped away and I imagined being in the previous century, before big cities and noise and lights. People's minds must have been clearer then, not so full of junk. And sharp, able to survive. My mind kept playing an endless tape of dumb stuff. "Coke, the pause that refreshes." "Be sociable, have a Pepsi." "Ho, ho, ho, Green Giant." "I'd walk a mile for a Camel." Jingles and songs, from soul to pop. When it switched off, it was heaven, but I also felt as though I were losing my identity. Then nature would console me again.

That last night, Saturday night, I decided not to lie down at all, but to sit under my cottonwood and be vigilant. An owl hooted nearby, and I imagined Grandma Winona coming to say hello. "Hello," I said.

I sat and watched the moon dance across the sky. I thought of how many millions of times it had done the same thing before. So reliable. Tied to the waves of the sea and a woman's monthly cycle. I sat through the pains in my back and cringed as my legs fell asleep. I imagined Grandma Winona massaging my legs, as she used to at night when they ached me to tears. "Growing pains," she would say, rubbing the pain away.

I closed my eyes and watched my breathing. It was something I seldom paid attention to, but now it felt like the most important thing in the world. Without this movement of air in and out, I would be dead in seconds. The deep breaths seemed as nourishing as food.

And I sat and sat, my eyes closed, a vessel waiting for the Great Spirit to fill me up. I heard drumming, or chants, and in my mind saw a shimmery form that got brighter and brighter. *Grandma Winona,* I said without speaking. *Is that you?*

"Yes, Dove," she said. "I'm glad you could come."

I smiled and listened for more.

"Don't doubt," she said. "Believe. I am always with you, and plenty of other spirits besides."

I nodded and felt a joy in my heart. Then she disappeared and I slowly opened my eyes. "I am never alone."

Overhead I made out the Big Dipper, or Big Bear, as Grandma Winona called it. And off to the side I saw a meteor streak through the sky like a chalk mark on a blackboard. I could actually hear it whizzing softly before it winked out. Full of peace, I fell asleep, and dreamed of the boy with the magical eyes.

When the Sunday sun opened my reluctant eyes, I felt more whole than I ever had. I got up and soaked my feet again and rinsed off my face and arms. My hunger and thirst were gone completely.

I spent the day sitting naked under the tree, doing as much nothing as I could, aware that this luxury of purification would soon be over, and I would get caught up in the distractions of life all over again.

I prayed for Mama and Daddy and Anna and Winona and Don and Inez and Frank and the soul of Marilyn Monroe, dead now a year. I prayed for Russia and the United States and the astronauts and for my friends and for Bernice and her sick mother and the whole wide world. When I was done I hadn't left anything out. I was way out in space, beyond the stars and planets and the sun, putting my arms around everything.

A wet tongue brought me back to earth. I jumped off the ground. "Bosco!"

My legs, which were sound asleep, buckled under me, and I crashed to the ground, where we tumbled and played with abandon. Then he howled and paced toward the west. I brushed myself off and looked at the position of the sun. "Time to go back, huh?" I said.

He barked, and I put on my stiff but dry clothes and took a final look around. Then we set off, going west, and followed the same path back home. By dusk we were nearly there, and I welcomed the idea of a cool shower, with soap. The little house at the edge of the field looked like home to me, and Bosco barked as soon as he saw it.

It seemed that Anna was running toward me forever, an image frozen now in my mind. I could not describe the joy I felt. "Thank God, thank God," she said, over and over. And when our arms finally met and we hugged so that we could not breathe, she seemed shorter somehow, and our eyes nearly on the same level.

· 14 ·

Summer was nearly over. In less than two weeks I would be leaving Anna and going back to school, to the eighth grade. It was hard to believe. I didn't know what to feel. Anna was nesting and waiting; now I was the one who craved adventure. But of course, Anna was simply getting ready for her own big adventure.

She still wasn't showing, at least not in her belly, and I sensed her trying on several occasions to confide her secret, then drawing back, so as not to jinx it. It would have ruined her to lose that baby.

I took over half of her work hours at Don's, and became one of the best waitresses he had ever had.

"You know," he said to me one day, winking, "you are as good as your aunt. Or, as good as she used to be before she started falling asleep!"

"It's just a phase with her," I said, smiling.

"Yes, I know," he said, squeezing my arm. "But

anytime you want a job here, you've got it. I don't care how young you are."

I enjoyed serving customers, a task that came naturally to me. A few times Don even let me cook, when Inez took sick with influenza, and he gave me a bonus in pay. I still hadn't seen the mysterious boy again, but I had never stopped thinking about him. Once or twice I thought I saw him in a passing car, but I was so busy now, with my job and Anna, that I didn't have time for wishing. I wrote Mama and told her that I had a job, and sent her half my paycheck. The rest I was keeping for college. Something inside of me was telling me that I was going to be a writer.

And then, the last week of August, Mama called. "I miss you," she said, not identifying herself. Her voice was deeper, more resonant.

"Mama! Is that you?"

"Yes," she said. "It is me, finally."

"I've been hoping you would call," I said, trying to hide my disappointment.

"I know," she said. "But I've been gone."

"I know. Anna told me when you called."

"Yes. The church ladies took care of the house — even painted the bathroom and brought in some plants — while Louis and I took a little vacation."

"You *and* Daddy? But —"

"Yes," she said. "Your daddy and I went off to Ardmore and stayed with his Great Aunt Bessie. After a while his Uncle Will and Aunt Loriene came by, and it was one big get-together. I guess the fresh air helped my condition, and now I only take one little nap every afternoon."

"Mama!" I said. Mama was out of bed!

"And Dovey, we're falling in love all over again! We feel like we just got back from a second honeymoon."

My heart pounded like a rabbit's, and I sat down on the floor, cradling the phone. Mama's words came out in a silky stream and didn't stop until her tears forced her to. She told me how she and Daddy had learned how to treat each other right by watching his uncle and aunt, how the family had talked day after day, and into the night, telling stories she had never heard. How some bond had tied them all together. How Daddy's Aunt Bessie had prepared some healing herbs for Mama, and said words over her. How Daddy told Mama he would go to Mass with her now whenever she asked. How her spirit had been wounded years ago when the doctor told her she would die if she tried to have any more children. How Daddy is going to AA meetings now on Wednesdays. How Anna had been Mama's strength this summer, sending her letters nearly every day (something I never realized Anna was doing). How proud she was of me and the woman I was becoming. How Daddy just last night got a job at the A&P.

"Dovey," she whispered, "I want to be your Mama again."

· 15 ·

After Uncle Wing died a year ago, Anna got most of his stuff. One afternoon I found a cigar box full of letters on the shelf in the living room. One was from Grandma Winona to Uncle Wing. It was dated June 1951.

> *Dear Wing,*
>
> *My dear brother, how I thought of you last night! Did you hear me calling your name? Never has a tornado come so close to harming us, and never have we all prayed so loudly together!*
>
> *I am glad you called me this morning from your vacation in North Dakota, but with the long distance, it was impossible to take the time to speak our hearts.*
>
> *The twister came up quickly, after dimpled, puffy, gray clouds had formed. We heard later that the winds got up to over 300 miles per hour!*

Warning whistles were wailing, and we heard that awful loud noise, like a train heading straight for you.

I rounded up Anna, her Harold, Louis, and carried Dovey myself. She's been walking for over a year now, and didn't want to be picked up. Mama is so hard of hearing that she kept ignoring me, until I pointed at the sky. Then, lo and behold, a long gray funnel dropped from the cloud bank, like a whirling carrot. Mama let out a whoop, and we all headed for the cellar.

We crouched around the little table and the kerosene lamp. It flickered and threatened to go out, my fingers were so unsteady with the match. My little radio went in and out, even though I just bought the batteries last week. Dovey crawled around unconcerned on the dirt floor and played with jars of vegetables that I had put up from last year. She hasn't learned yet that the updraft from those terrible funnels can suck up houses, animals, and cars into the air and carry them hundreds of feet. Remember Papa telling us how in Oklahoma, he saw a tornado lift frogs and fish from ponds, then drop them down onto people's heads in the city? And the rain of blood, when the rain mixed with clay and then fell back to earth? He told me he once saw a waterspout as the funnel pulled water up from a lake.

None of this happened to us last night, but all these things passed through my mind. We prayed and cried that this would not be our last night on earth. I prayed especially for my children and Dovey and Harold, who hold the hope for our future. Nothing is sadder than for an old person to survive her offspring.

So the noise continued, the wind and the rain. We heard a loud explosion, and learned a while later that our neighbor's barn had exploded. Not one board was left standing. Even Dovey got scared from the noise, and tried to nurse at her mama's breasts, which have been dry for several months. The next day Anna found a drinking straw that had been driven into one of our trees. It stuck out at a ninety-degree angle! Destruction lay on all sides, but we were spared, except for two chickens that must have gotten sucked up and deposited elsewhere.

My dear Wing, we have been given another chance. A chance to live another day, help our neighbors as they rebuild their lives, and live closer to the Spirit. I am glad most of my family surrounded me, the way it should be.

Dovey is interrupting me now to say that she wants you to bring her a horse of her own. "Horsie" was one of the first words she spoke. She seems to love them as much as you do.

Well, I have to start dinner. Louis has just chopped the head off a chicken, and the rest will be left to me. Come back soon, and keep us in your heart.

Your loving sister,
Winona

· 16 ·

Troy was back home again. I was the first to remember, as we sat down to flapjacks and sausages.
It was Friday, August 30, and Hugh Downs was
prophesying a good day. His kind eyes looked
beyond what Grandma Winona used to call the Big
City out to our little home in the wheat. Troy
watched the *Today Show* whenever he got a chance.

"It's today," I said cheerfully, looking at Troy as
he filled my coffee cup.

"Of course, little flower," he said with a smile.
"Isn't it always?"

Anna laughed and then glanced at the calendar.
"Joe's family's reunion!" she said. "Why, we better
get moving. We have a long drive ahead of us." She
patted my head. "Now don't fill up too much, because they usually have quite a spread of food set
out."

I pushed one of my sausage patties back onto the
serving plate.

"Have you ever been, Troy?" I asked.

"Just once," he said. "And I put on a good five pounds while I was there." He squeezed his belly, which was firm and flat as a board. Then he leaned over to Anna and rubbed his head on her hair like a cat.

"But the best part was that that was the day I first met my Anna."

Anna kissed him on the earlobe and put her arm around his shoulders. "Best thing that's happened in a long while," she said.

Now that Troy was living with us, Anna was bright and energetic again.

The phone rang, for the first time in several days. It had been one of the few silent parts of the house.

"For you, love," said Anna.

She scraped the rest of her breakfast into Bosco's bowl and rinsed off her fingers. I went up behind her and bravely kissed her on the neck. She smelled like Troy.

"Dovey, Dovey," she said, without turning around, then began humming an endless medley of love songs, leading off with "Fly Me to the Moon."

Troy was talking and talking, to some kind of counselor. I thought maybe it was to Father John, maybe about the marriage classes Catholics are supposed to take before getting married. But Anna never even mentioned going to Mass anymore, and didn't seem interested in religion.

"Haskell," Troy said. "Yes." His voice was confident. "The plan has changed. I'll be able to start this fall. So you think the science department there is good? Okay."

Keeping a secret in this house was next to impossible, and I was starting to wonder why people even bothered.

I put on my favorite red shirt and my only pair of jeans and walked around the front yard. My spirits were as breezy and clear as the sky above.

I was almost the age when many of the females of the world got married and had children. My grandmother, mother, and Anna had had babies by the age of seventeen.

Bosco snaked ahead of me, his rear end badly in need of alignment. He shot off after a prairie dog, and continued to bark at it long after the animal had made a hasty retreat down its hole.

My jeans felt tighter than usual, making me walk like John Wayne. Anna's kitchen radio blared out Paul Anka's "Diana," my favorite girl's name in the world. Leaping to the only available branch of the oak standing next to me, I hung by my knees and swayed like a pendulum. Marking time, first quickly, then slowing down until I was nearly still. Bosco whined in confusion at my state, and licked my face, now red as a beet.

"Are we ready?" yelled Anna. The radio was silent. She had a huge watermelon in her arms.

"Reddy Kilowatt," said Troy, emerging from the front door, all crisp and handsome in khakis and black leather boots. He carried two six-packs of beer.

"Yes, ma'am!" I shouted, looking down at the clouds. Anna smiled and shook her head as she closed the door behind her.

We piled into the car like bandits, full of energy and in strong alliance. Anna started off the first car game. The category was animals.

"Slug," she said. I searched for an animal whose name began with the last letter.

"Giraffe," I said, poking Troy on the shoulder.

"Elephant," he said.

"Tiger," said Anna. "And you only get five seconds."

"Rat," I said, my heart beating fast.

"Thrush," said Troy.

Anna snorted. "Hog."

"Gook!" I yelled.

Anna and Troy turned around and frowned at me. "Hey," said Troy.

"Look it up!" I protested. "The spotted gook!" But I was only half sure that a real animal existed by that name. Now that I thought about it, I'd only heard the word used to refer to the short people my school bus driver had shot at in Korea.

"Don't make fun of Orientals," said Anna. She stroked Troy's left temple. "Why, look at that slant."

"Just got a good slant on the world, is all," he said. "And anyway, they think that the North American Indians probably came here from China, walking across the Bering Strait land bridge."

"We are Chi–a–nese, if you please," I sang.

"We are Chi–a–nese, if you don't please," echoed Troy and Anna.

We must have played a dozen car games as we flew south through Kansas and into Oklahoma. Thank goodness there were no patrol cars around. We passed counties like Nowata, Cherokee, Muskogee, Macintosh, and Atoka. Troy told me that a Choctaw chief, Allen Wright, named Oklahoma after the Choctaw words for "red" and "man."

"Summer is an Indian time," said Troy. "We put up with the cold and keep to ourselves then, but when the season turns and the land warms up, we can't hold still. You've just got to go!"

"Yes," said Anna. "Go to your people. Even if some of them drive you crazy."

Troy leaned back and closed his eyes. The wind blew sections of his hair around. "My Cheyenne great-grandfather used to tell us about the great sunflower wars, where the boys would turn the plants into lances and pretend to drive the blue-coat soldiers from their lands. He's an old man now, but he still talks about that."

Anna laughed. "And Winona used to take Louis

and me to prayer meetings in the summer, and grad-
uations and powwows and gourd dances."

"The Sun Dance is the one I wish I could have
seen," said Troy.

My ears perked up. "You mean that gross one
where they hang the guy way up, by the skin of his
chest?" I shuddered and slumped back in my seat.

"Sit up," said Troy. "For the Cheyennes, the Sun
Dance is called Standing Against the Enemy, and if
you can't do that, you just might get yourself killed.
The dance showed the people what bravery is."

I sat up and felt a pain in my chest. "Yes, sir," I
said.

He messed up my hair and punched my arm.

· 17 ·

"Oklahoma's scenery isn't dramatic like those desert and mountain westerns you see," said Anna. "It doesn't have the Grand Canyon, but if you look deeper you can see deer, raven, and a lot more. And the soil is like the Chickasaw soil of the South — red and yellow-brown clay in the hills, and black earth along the rivers. They stuck to the forests, mostly. Open areas of the west scared them back then."

Troy nodded. "There's an Oklahoma legend that says certain Indians can become transparent, turn into a leaf, or hitch a ride on a bird's wing."

"Why, the Indian lawyer in a three-piece suit can easily turn into a feathered championship dancer," said Anna. "Or an elected law enforcer can go into his office the morning after a peyote meeting. Or a university professor goes to see his medicine doctor because a witch is haunting him. We have two heritages now."

Anna looked at me in the rearview mirror. "Remember that fat redhead guy that started coming to eat at Don's a few days ago?"

"Mr. Ludlow?" I said. "That creep who's always bragging?"

"Ludlow. That's him," said Anna. "Well, the other day I heard him going on about his tribal genealogy like he was the son of a famous chief or something. Come to find out he's got one two-hundred-fifty-sixth Indian blood." She cackled. "Then there's my niece Mary who begged her history teacher not to tell any of her classmates that she's Indian."

"Strange world," said Troy, looking off.

"This part is getting familiar," said Anna, pointing to a line of trees up ahead. We were going seventy-five.

"All *right!*" yelled Troy. "Just another few minutes, Dovey."

I smoothed my hair and looked ahead. We were approaching a four-way intersection, with a police car pulling up to the stop sign at our right. *Uh oh,* I thought, as we came to a stop.

He honked loud and long at us.

"Damn," said Anna. "He saw how fast I was going."

Troy leaned out his window. "Dennis!" he yelled. "Hey, man! Are you going to the reunion?"

Dennis reminded me of Dennis Wilson from the Beach Boys. "Well, if I'm interested in staying alive," the patrolman said. "Even though I'm only a distant cousin, twice removed, Joe would kill me if I missed it. See you in a couple, when I get off duty."

Anna sighed with relief.

"And by the way," Dennis said, "you might want to watch that speedometer. There might be a cop or two in this county."

"Right," said Troy, jabbing Anna with his elbow. "Hey, that's the Blue River." He looked back at me and said, "Bernice's family is the Leflores. The family allotment is right over there." He pointed straight ahead. "Along the river. Do you know about Tishomingo?"

"The Chickasaw Nation's capital," I said. Grandma Winona had told me about it long ago. I liked the sound of it, and thought it might make a good name for a dog.

"Well, it's just a few miles away. And the Choctaws go there for Labor Day homecoming. They call it the Choctaw holiday."

"We might take you there, Dovey," said Anna, "if your school doesn't start before then."

"Okay," I said, looking around. It felt like home, somehow. Not my home in Lawrence, but another kind I'd never felt before. There were tall cedars here, and impressive granite rocks.

"We're here!" said Anna.

We followed a two-lane dirt road that curved to the left and stopped just before a small two-story frame house.

"Wow," I whispered. Ahead of us were parked dozens of vehicles, from big mobile vans to VW bugs. A crowd of people milled around, of all ages, from newborns to a couple who must have been in their nineties. I was surprised at the number of Indians in the crowd; in fact, it was mostly Indians.

Anna parked between two pickups and we got out.

"Lord!" said Troy, pointing to a large yellow John Deere crane which was raising and lowering into place a bunch of picnic tables.

"Lord, Lord," said Anna.

Troy carried the watermelon, and gave Anna and me each a six-pack to carry.

"Troy!" said an old man with a wide smile and stained teeth. "Just caught me a catfish." He stood next to a portable butane burner that had a big black kettle on it.

"Johnny!" said Troy. They hugged one another. "You remember Anna?"

Johnny nodded. "Nobody forgets Anna Derry-saw." He took her hand.

"And this is her niece, Dovey."

"Dovey?" he said. "Pleased to meet you." His hand was leathery and warm, and I enjoyed the feel of it. "Cousin Charles here is cooking *pahsofa*, Dovey," he said. "Corn and pork."

I shook Charles's hand. His pot sat on a wood fire, and smelled like heaven. "This pot is a hundred years old," he said. "We use it every time the Leflores get together."

I was distracted by a carload of dark-skinned men who yelled to us as they drove by. "Some idiot forgot the cornmeal!" one said. "Back in a few."

We wound our way through gangs of little boys running up and down the riverbank, one of them holding up a long string of poison ivy. A circle of little girls whispered among themselves and giggled.

"Troy! Anna!" said a woman with a face as old as the hills. "Come see the twins! They were born just five days ago. I'm a great-grandmother!"

People were coming toward us and welcoming us, as if we had just entered the gates of heaven. I was dizzy with delight.

Anna let out several whoops and hollers.

"There you are!" she yelled, opening her arms wide. "Want you to meet my niece."

Troy held my head with his right palm as though it were a basketball. I looked at the woman approaching us. She was as lovely as the Indian princess that lived on the moon, tall and dark with two thick braids pulled together in back. Her eyes were all pupils, and every movement part of some graceful dance. I stood and stared, faced with an impossible ideal which I ached to attain.

"Why, you look just like some old photos of me!" she said without a trace of insincerity.

"I — do?" I offered her my hand.

"Dovey, this is Bernice," said Anna. "Bernice — Dovey." My jaw dropped. Bernice was an Indian? But how could she be the mother of Joe's pale, freckled boys?

"Quite a tribe here," said Troy, smiling at Bernice.

"Yes," she said. "Isn't it great?"

"How's your mom?" Anna asked.

"She pulled through like a trooper. I'll be going back home tomorrow."

"Thank God," said Anna. "Say, where's that Joe fella?"

"Over there," said Bernice, "stoking the fire."

We all walked toward the huge barbecue pit, on which beef, venison, and chicken roasted, sending out mouthwatering smells. Joe looked up and greeted us with a big smile.

"Met my wife?" he asked, putting his arm around Bernice tightly.

"Yes, sir," I nodded.

"Aren't I lucky?" he asked. "I married Bernice three years ago, after my first wife passed away. Never thought I'd feel this way. Happy as a cat."

"Oh, mush," said Anna. "You always were the smiling type."

"Not like this, Anna," said Joe, nuzzling Bernice's long, soft neck. "I'm telling you true."

Some others approached us, offering plates and

warm handshakes. "The food starts over there," a middle-aged Choctaw said to us, "and winds around quite a ways. Go help yourself."

"This is a mixed crowd, see," Troy told me. "The Choctaw and Chickasaw half is from Bernice's side, the blonds and redheads from Joe's."

Anna laughed and headed for the feast. Her eye had spotted two of her favorites — pemmican, made from dried meat, grease, and berries; and sassafras tea.

People would stand up and give speeches about the Leflores, the Blue River, the sharing of happiness and pain.

I wandered among the noises and smells, half expecting to find kin of my own. Two rows had lined up around the picnic tables, and I joined one, overwhelmed at the variety of foods. On my plate I placed a chicken thigh, a slice of venison, a scoop of squash, some beans, fried bread, and an ear of corn. Two Indian ministers stood up and said grace in two languages.

As I relaxed into their rhythm and strange sounds, I felt a presence from across the table. It was so strong that my hand began to shake, and when I looked up I saw two hauntingly familiar eyes.

· 18 ·

It was the dark-eyed boy I had seen at Don's. Or thought I had seen. Now I knew it hadn't been a dream. We stared boldly without words or movement, until one of Joe's boys nudged my elbow and pointed at some blueberry cobbler.

"Try that!" he said. "Me and my brother made it."

I plunked back to reality and put some cobbler on top of my chicken. Then Joe and Bernice came over and pulled me in their direction. "Sit with us, Dove," said Joe.

I sat down on a large navy wool blanket and looked around. The young man was fast slipping away again.

I pointed excitedly at him as he was just about to blend in with a dark-skinned cluster.

"Who is he?" I asked Bernice, trying to sound nonchalant.

"Who's who?" she said.

"That boy, the one over there with the gray sweatshirt." Bernice squinted into the sun.

"Oh, that's Vine," she said. "My favorite little cousin. He's also an artist. You'll love him."

She stuck her fingers into her mouth and let out a loud whistle. Vine turned around. As he walked toward me I felt flushed and naked.

I cleared off a space at the corner of the blanket and scooted next to Troy. Vine sat down and smiled a smile to melt my heart.

"Vine," said Bernice, "I want you to meet Eleanor." Vine sat down and offered me his olive-colored hand.

"We call her Dovey," said Anna.

Troy nodded to the boy as he gulped down his venison. "Vine."

"Vine lives down the road a ways from us. Helps us in the summer with baling," said Bernice. Vine nodded.

"But he's really an artist," she said proudly. "A painter like you wouldn't believe."

I looked at his face, self-composed and honest. His nose was prominent and his cheekbones sharp. And in his black eyes a magnet that pulled me inside. I realized that my hand was still clasping his, and he hadn't pulled away. Gently, reluctantly, I released my grip.

"So, you still planning to go to Haskell Indian Institute in a couple of years?" asked Troy. "I hear their art department's really good."

"Yes, sir," said Vine. "And it'll be great meeting other tribes from all over the country."

Troy smiled. "Well, I'll tell you all about it come September! I'm going to start on my science degree!"

"No kidding, man?" said Vine. "That's too much!"

It was too much for me. Something was stirring inside me, and it wasn't from the beans. I wondered if I looked as overwhelmed as I felt.

"Dove," said Vine. "So would you mind?"

My mind was floating around. "Mind?"

"Yes," he said. "Mind if I sketched you. Out there. In the cornfields."

The others were talking loudly among themselves, leaving Vine and me in our private bubble. He pulled a small pad and pencil from his hip pocket.

I shook my head. "No."

"Back in June," he said softly, "when I saw you in the diner, I thought you were a vision."

I nodded again. "Me, too."

"But this is real, isn't it?" he asked.

We smiled and left the crowd behind. His hand softly cradled the small of my back as we entered the tall rows that now reminded me of a cathedral.

He told me where to sit, then allowed me the luxury of staring into his deep eyes for what seemed an eternity, as he drew quickly and assuredly. I was as nervous as a cat. Or, as my grandmother used to say, "nervous as a cat in a room full of rocking chairs." My knees knocked and I kept forgetting to breathe. But I wanted to be brave and bold as Vine was.

"Your spirit is very beautiful," he said at last, handing me a drawing of a striking young woman, confident and open. I studied it in amazement.

"Keep it," he said, smiling.

"Oh, Vine!" A tear leaped from my eye and we stood facing one another. He pulled me in close, in an embrace unlike any I had ever experienced. I felt a wholeness, an excitement that exceeded my wildest dreams. Lady Chatterley had nothing on me.

"Listen," he said, "there's a wonderful Appaloosa in that field over there. Do you want to go ride him with me?"

My heart leaped, but then I thought of my arm, and what Mama would say if she knew I was riding again. It was a chance I would have to take.

"Oh, yes!" I said. "I love to ride."

We got permission from Anna and Joe, and went to bridle the horse. He whinnied a warm hello. Vine and I hopped on him bareback and rode all over, past the picnic area, the swimming hole, the corn and wheat fields, the chickens and cows, to the far pond. The wind blew in our faces as we held on to one another and to the stallion. It seemed he could sprout wings and fly us to the moon. After what seemed like hours, we took him back and groomed him with a curry comb, laughing and panting together.

Vine and I returned to the reunion, radiant, holding hands. We sat down, Indian style, on Anna and Troy's blanket, our knees overlapping. Anna winked at me and smiled.

"Guess what?" said Troy. "Anna just said she'd marry me!" His voice carried throughout the crowd, and everyone started clapping and whistling. They got up and bowed. Someone threw a sunflower at Anna. She picked it up and put it behind her ear.

The noise died down, and everyone went back to eating.

"And Dovey, we want you to be in our wedding," said Anna.

I hugged her and kissed her on the cheek. "Oh, Anna."

Vine and Troy joined the big bear hug and we all swayed together, laughing and crying at the same time.

As the sun went down, and whippoorwills called, everyone started singing hymns in Choctaw, Chickasaw, and English. Goodbyes progressed from the picnic area to the house to the insides of cars and trucks, everyone reluctant to let this day end. Gossip intermingled with tears and laughter, and a final promise to meet again next year.

A horn honked impatiently for Vine. He looked

at me and touched my arm. "I'll call you tomorrow. When I get off work." I nodded and wondered how I would ever be able to wait until then.

Bernice came up and hugged Troy and Anna. When she got to me, she whispered, "I told you you'd like Vine."

Joe and the kids came up and shook hands. "Hey, you two," he said, "don't forget that my next-door neighbor is an ordained minister. Why, he could marry you right in the middle of my wheat fields!"

I sat in the back seat as Anna drove Troy and me home. Our headlights formed two white tunnels through the darkness, and the hours flew by. Drifting in and out of sleep, catching bits of their conversation, I gave in to a pleasant tiredness, and slept for several hours. When I roused and looked out the window, I could see a clock on a Conoco gas station that said two-thirty. I turned on the overhead lamp to look at the map. Highway 59 at Garnett. We would be home in no time.

Troy snuggled close to Anna, and spoke softly in her ear. "You know what, Anna?" he said. "One of the Choctaw elders reminded me today of something."

"Oh?"

"Yeah. He said that last month was the Moon of the Budding Trees and Flowers."

"Yes," she said. "July."

A chill went down my spine.

"And now," he said, "August is the Moon —"

Anna chimed in, a distant memory now returning to her:

". . . When the Berries Are Good."

I smiled and suddenly noticed, in the crotch of my jeans, an ever-widening stain of blood. Flaming and new, the berry juices of a ripening woman. I turned off the light and gathered my things together. Yes, tonight Anna and I would have many things to share, woman to woman.